The World of Winifred Dorfinkle

by

Peter Glassman

Dedicated to my grandchildren who have continued to stimulate my storylines, which have developed into published novels, short stories, and magazine articles.

This is a work of fiction. The events, characters, and situations are from the author's imagination. However, the story may also just not have happened…yet.

Peter Glassman MD, PhD

Author's Note

The World of Winifred Dorfinkle could well be The world of Anyone. I came from a mixed marriage wherein my father was Jewish and my mother Roman Catholic. Ethnically, my father was a product of Russian parentage. My mother was the result of an Italian mating. As children we grew up Jewish since my mother was excommunicated for marrying outside of her faith. She did convert to Judaism. My father maintained that as long as God was part of any religion it didn't matter which one you chose as long as you felt comfortable with it.

My basic theme is to depict the possibilities of not only religious denominations, but overcoming the barriers they impose. In this book, Winifred Dorfinkle is a drama student in New York City with a crush on a Catholic Priest at St. Patrick's Cathedral. Winnie's life is fraught with always labeled as Jewish because of her name. Father Forbish Nesbitt is a celibate catholic priest. They meet at the confessionals. Winnie has an active free-floating mind with visions of becoming a successful actress. Father Nesbitt wants only to maintain peace in the lives of his constituents. Not only does love spark in both, but life and death issues complicate their aspirations. Father Nesbitt is a former Navy SEAL who has been targeted by the sole survivor of his last combat action in Iraq. Choices abound as they do in all lives—especially with the never-ending outrageous phenomena that exist in New York City. If a reader wants fun mixed with adventure and the serious, then please enter The World of Winifred Dorfinkle.

Peter Glassman MD, PhD

Chapter 1
Guilt

Her name is Winifred Dorfinkle. Boyfriends, when she has one, call her Winnie, at least around New York City's Thespian Drama Academy. Girl friends, which she always has, call her Winnie or Dorf. No one calls her Finkle except Claudia. Claudia's her mother's red and orange Macaw. The bird calls her Finkle. She doesn't consciously call her Finkle. Her Aunt Lisa from Massachusetts visited and stayed with them for a few days. Aunt Lisa always greets Winnie with, "Hello, Finkle." For some reason Claudia absorbed the words into her tape recorder mind. Now anytime anyone addresses Claudia with "Hello, Claudia," Claudia responds with "Hello, Finkle."

She's on her way to St. Patrick's Cathedral, around the corner, sort of, from her drama school. It's actually a few blocks. Winnie likes to keep her mind pure and purged of any feelings like guilt, shame, regrets, or remorse. Any dark, negative, or wrongful thought affects her performance as a potential actress. The way she does it is with confession. Winifred Dorfinkle is a Catholic. Her father's Jewish and her mother's Catholic. Only one clergyman, a Catholic Priest, would marry them...but only if the kids were brought up Catholic. Winnie's not devout, but enough to believe there's a hell, and for her hell would be living a life as other than being in the theatre. She used to think it would be nice to be Jewish, but then she would never have met Father Nesbbit.

St. Pat's is a massive church. It has classical old world church anatomy. In books on church architecture, you'll find St. Patrick's of New York City, usually in a full color photo. Even the front entrance is awesome. The bronze doors rise so high, it's hard to imagine anyone that tall. Even two Abraham Lincolns standing on each others shoulders would have clearance.

One of the doors is usually unlocked on non-Catholic Holy Days, like today. The one on the left is always open to anyone. Anyone but bums and beggars who just want to come out of bad weather. St. Pat's has a bouncer for that. He's not really a bouncer. Father Nesbitt calls him a caretaker. His name is Montague Kelp. He keeps the sidewalks clear of snow, ice, or any street filth that accumulates—which it does every day.

As she approaches St. Patrick's she can't help think of the caretaker. *Kelp, what a name. The only kelp I knew before I met "Caveman Monty" was the seaweed that grows in the ocean like tall redwoods.* The metal door is easy to open. She enters, and Kelp magically appears to make sure she's not a bum. He disappears just as magically.

᙭

It's 8:30 on this crisp cold October Thursday morning. Winnie's goal is to be at St. Pat's by nine, to be sure to get Father Nesbbit. He's a young Priest and prone to flexible modern interpretation of Papal direction. Which means, he talks with you rather than just recite penitence for perceived sins. He rarely sentences his acolytes to a million "Hail Marys". Instead, handsome Father Nesbbit, who Darryl, one of Winnie's ex-boyfriends, once called Father Nebbish, discusses the positives of any confessed imagined "wrongs".

The light on the confessional arch just turned green and it's Winnie's turn. She takes a deep breath. *Well, here goes.* Her spirits lift as she sees the card for her confessor— Father Forbish Nesbbit. *Forbish, what a first name. Maybe that's the reason why some call him Father Nebbish. The word Nebbish means a "nobody", a meaningless non-entity. Maybe I was too hasty dumping Darryl.*

Winnie's still a little nervous as she sits down on the wooden chair in the darkened cell. It smells of cigar smoke. Nesbbit doesn't smoke, and she could never imagine him with a cigar. *No, it must be from one of the two women who went before her. The last one looked like a hooker.* She could be the smoker, she considers, but changes her thought midstream. *I bet her last trick puffed on a Cohiba® while they were in the sack.* She blushes as she thinks she's about to be with Father Nesbitt, even if she can't see him through the mesh separator.

The slide from the divider moves ending in a final "click", which is a signal for her to speak. *I better take off my hat and let my shiny brown hair fall to my shoulders, just in case he's able to see me. I mean, I really look like a teenager on a ski slope with my bright orange bobble hat with the three red yarn pompoms on top.*

After a deep breath, like when she goes swimming, She begins. "Father, forgive me for I have sinned. It's been two weeks since my last confession."

"Winnie, you rarely commit what the Pope would call a real sin–at least, in the past two years since you've been coming to St. Patrick's."

Nesbbit breaks anonymity in the confessional, only with regulars like Winnie. Winnie fantasizes that it would be wonderful if he did this with just her. She dreams of being someone special to him. She uses a somber voice from her acting training, "I really did it this time, Father. Just remembering my dream is a constant distraction from my studies and performance at the drama school."

"Let's hear it, Winnie. Just breathe slowly, swallow, and tell me about it. Let it all out."

He has a deep, mellow voice. *He really could be a movie star with his good looks and penetrating projection.*

She breathes an audible sigh and swallows, just as he said and begins."Father Nesbbit, I had a vivid dream a few nights ago after I performed an important acting part."

"Anything done as an actress, on stage, or in a play, is not considered a deliberate wrong or sinful act, Winnie."

"It doesn't have anything to do with the theatre." She paused—maybe too long—but he doesn't say anything. "Okay, here goes. Father, Monday night I woke up having had this unusual dream. I mean, unusual for me…sort of. It seemed so real, I actually thought it happened. I was afraid I committed a terrible act on myself. It wasn't an injury or related to any role I ever played."

"Winnie, just come out with it. Externalize any self-defiling thoughts, dreams, and ideas. You'll immediately feel better. And knowing you, it most likely will not come under the category of something against God's will."

His words are soothing and give Winnie courage. "Father, I dreamed I violated myself multiple times by having impure thoughts. Oh, Father, what will you think of me. I can't…"

"Winnie, your words will never leave this confessional."

"All right, Father. I dreamt I had intense and enjoyable sex with a very large banana."

Chapter 2
Bananas

Winnie was more guilt-ridden after the confession. She really must tell Father Nesbitt about bananas. She wasn't really obsessed with bananas. It was her doctor. *Yes, I must tell him about Dr. Potts, but how to do it.*

Health-wise she's usually okay. It was her physical appearance as a future actress and current drama student at the Thespian Drama Academy that was important. So, she found this really cool MD who practices as an Addictionologist. Winnie wasn't addicted to any substance, but addictionologists treat being overweight as an addiction or eating disorder. She attended a lecture given by him entitled, "Sculpting the body through diet".

Dr. Myron Potts is a notable around New York City. He claims half his patients are people obsessed with maintenance of an ideal body weight and proper anatomical dimensions. Potts says half of that patient group are those in the theatre, aspiring to be in the theatre, models, single women, or gay and lesbian couples. *I'll tell Father Nesbitt about Potts first and get to the bananas eventually.*

She remembered her first visit with Dr. Potts. For some reason she was nervous. His office nurse weighed her on a balance scale. The nurses's name is Gertrude Pickles—Mrs. Gertrude Pickles.

"Well, Ms. Dorfinkle, for a height of five-foot-four you're at your ideal calculated body weight of 120 pounds...in clothes...without shoes." Pickles entered the data on a laptop. She smiled at Winnie's stare at her computer. "These days paper files have been replaced by electronic devices."

"It's the same at school, with computers I mean. And as for what I look like now, Mrs. Pickles, I bet I could say the same for you. You look properly proportioned." Pickles had an attractive face, a pointy stand-up bosom, narrow waistline, and a bottom like Winnie's, which was far from protuberant.

"Well, Ms. Dorfinkle, I'm upfront about myself. I believe in Dr. Potts' medical practice. He literally has helped all his weight-patients achieve their goals. I'm one of his patients. However, I came to Dr. Potts after I had a boob job, tummy tuck, and butt implants. I looked good for about six months after my surgeries were done. Then I started to gain weight and ended up looking like the Michelin Tire Man. I was lumpy everywhere. Dr. Potts got me back to what you see before you." She twirled around and stuck out her chest and behind.

"I'm an acting student at the Thespian Drama Academy. I want to maintain my shape and never get fat." The words just came out. "You can call me Winnie."

"As I said...Winnie...Dr. Potts can most probably help keep you on the right track. That is, if you comply with the program he designs for your lifestyle. You can call me Gert."

"Gert, can I ask you why Dr. Potts has a nutritional healthcare practice when he's an Addictionologist? Does he have drug and alcohol addicts coming here too?"

She smiled, "Dr. Potts loves to answer that question, so I'll leave that to him."

Pickles handed her a paper patient gown, the kind with an opening on the back. She pointed to the examination table. "Remove everything except your watch and jewelry." Pickles gave her a sheepish grin and said, "Put on the gown covering your front and don't tie the back. I'll be here with Dr. Potts for your evaluation." She pressed a button on the telephone base for Dr. Potts to enter.

Winnie was now all alone. Well, not really, she was wrapt in her thoughts. Whenever she was alone, like this or on the subway, even when it's full of people, she let her mind wander. Mostly, she thought of her lines for her next scene at the Thespian. Other times her thoughts were of Father Nesbitt. *What a waste of a good, handsome, intelligent, desirable, and ,of course, single man. I can't help my infatuation. And, above all, I'm hopeful. That's because of my dad. When I was in high school, I was forever approached by the Jewish girls. Sarah Bloom was the first.*

"Dorfinkle, huh? Cute name. Are you going to join the BBG?" Sara Bloom asked.

"BBG? What's that?" She stared at Bloom's overdeveloped round boobs.

"The B'nai Brith Girls, it's a Jewish sorority for high schoolers. You are Jewish aren't you? I mean with a name like Dorfinkle?"

"Oh, yeah, my dad's Jewish, my mom's Catholic. Our religion is Catholic. I'm Catholic."

"Wow. Too bad, that means you can't join. But we can still be friends."

That was the start of an ongoing high school friendship with Sara Bloom. She taught Winnie all about Judaism, stuff her dad never told her. Her digressing into reverie left as the door to the exam room opened after a light knock.

ى

Dr. Myron Potts entered wearing a long unbuttoned white coat. It was open enough to reveal a bright red vest, pink shirt, and yellow tie. His large black eyeglass frames on a prominent nose and thinning disorderly, early balding, tan hair reminded her of one of her favorite acting-directors—Woody Allen. He smiled after looking at the laptop Pickles gave him.

"Ms. Dorfinkle, I'm Dr. Potts, my dear. You're interested in a weight control consultation I see."

He sounds like Woody Allen. He's much taller though. Winnie clutched her paper front. "Yes, Dr. Potts, I'm a drama student and future actress. I need to have a dietary lifestyle where I'll keep my figure." *My God even with his smile he looks like an idiot, like Woody Allen sometimes does.*

"Ms. Dorfinkle, I have to say, in all honesty and sincerity, that what you have is a thoroughly correct and wholesome attitude. Yes indeed, my dear"

This is uncanny, Woody Allen talks like that on screen. "Doctor, I believe it's easier to maintain my figure than have to remodel it after getting fat, you know."

He laughed and his wispy hair moved out from his temples. "Like I said, you come across with the correct deportment and drive to fit into one of my food education pathways. Yes indeed, my dear."

He extended his palm to the room's walls which were resplendent with pictures of food. Winnie hadn't noticed them when she was sitting here by her lonesome. She scanned the four walls. They reminded her of the Panera Bread Restaurant she goes to with framed art containing loaves of bread. *Panera even has a picture of Stonehenge where the large rocks are all gigantic pillars of what looks like sourdough bread.*

"I'll explain first, and if you still wish to continue here, a physical examination, lab work, and your family history are next."

At this point Pickles received the laptop back from Potts and began entering some stuff. She gave Winnie a nod of approval.

I've passed the first impression acceptance by the eminent Dr. Woody, I mean, Dr. Myron Potts.

He sat on the shiny metal stool at the end of the exam table. Placing his hands on both his knees exposed his grey and black checkered slacks. He began. "First, may I call you by your first name. Weight maintenance is such a personal thing that patient first names seem to eliminate any hurdles of resistance to treatment with formality of a Mr., Mrs. or Ms."

She nodded in agreement. "You can call me Winnie."

"Very nice. my dear, I do insist, however, that you refer to me as Dr. Potts to foster creditability of our program for you."

Winnie gave a positive nod.

"As you look around this room, Winnie, I have displayed photos of foods of a wide variety of ethnic and, I, hasten to add, healthy, bills of fare. These are palatable foodstuffs containing protein, carbohydrate, and, yes, some fat. Vitamins, amino acids, and intermediate fatty acids are inherent to zero weight gain." He paused to look at her absorbing expression. "I'm not giving a course in nutrition here, just throwing out that what we do is medically and ethically based on fact. You'll retain this knowledge as our visits continue. Especially you will learn, today, I might add, that some foods actually inhibit appetite, my dear Winnie."

Visits? More than One? I actually expected it. Winnie nodded for him to proceed.

"There exists in nature a wealth of edible things that with proper amount, kind, and timing, will become a lifestyle to achieve your goals. By timing, I like to speak of the British. Their biggest meal is breakfast. They partake of a moderate lunch. But dinner, and this is paramount Winnie, dinner is the smallest meal of the day. And why?" He paused. "I thought you'd never ask, my dear."

I didn't ask. This is more Woody Allen stuff, especially all these "my dears".

He continued, "After breakfast and lunch, a person is ambulatory, mobile, and exercising just by moving about during the day. In other words, we use up our calories. What happens after dinner? Usually nothing really physical as most people just go to bed after watching television. All those dinner calories turn into extra tissue…fatty tissue."

Wow. This stuff I can understand.

"Now, the lab work will give us a baseline for your normal status. Every six months we repeat it to make sure your vital organ systems are still performing correctly." He looked behind her to Pickles. "At this time if you wish to proceed, we will complete an examination and obtain a blood and urine specimen."

How is he going to obtain my urine?

❧

Dr. Potts performed her physical exam with complete regard to modesty. He used the paper gown to uncover and re-cover each part he examined. Pickles maneuvered the gown. At the end, Pickles handed her a "specimen cup" and motioned to the bathroom.

So much for my fear of dispensing my bladder contents in some invasive way.

"Okay, Winnie, you go through that door to Dr. Potts' office. You'll give him your family, travel, and dietary history."

The office was an eight by twelve conservatively furnished room with a dark mahogany desk, a tan sofa facing the desk, and two cushioned chairs at each desk corner. A Persian rug covered the floor and pale yellowish bamboo grass cloth wallpaper received his diplomas and certifications. Behind him two feet higher than his head was a very large framed photo.

Potts declared he was satisfied with her exam and would go over her lab work next time, which was in two weeks. He caught her staring at the large picture above his head.

"You may come to appreciate that photo as you continue here. As I mentioned between our six-month visits, Mrs. Pickles and I conduct group education about food and food addiction. I'm sure you know of some items that produce cravings such as chocolate and coffee. We talk about this during our tutorials, which are given once every two weeks at lunchtime and some evenings."

"So what about that picture, Dr. Potts. I find it most interesting. It even fits in with the color scheme of your office." She really found it weird or funny actually. It fit in with her Woody Allen image.

He swiveled his chair to look at it. "There are some foods, as I mentioned, that can suppress appetite. And the banana, like the enlarged picture here, is one of them. You'll learn about this in detail at your first tutorial." He handed her a large manila envelope. "The materials in this packet will be your introduction to your performance here. Please read them as they will be the subject of your next visit when we go over you lab work. Do you have any questions at this point. Questions from patients add to the success of our program."

"Yes, do you also treat drug addicts? I mean your specialty is Addictionology."

Potts sat back, "I hear that query often, Winnie my dear. I started out treating mostly people of all ages addicted to alcohol and drugs. My practice, at that time, with overweight and morbid obesity was small. As my alcoholic, opiate, and cocaine dependent people stopped using their substances, guess what?"

Winnie liked the give and take method, "They gained weight."

Potts beamed, "Absolutely correct, my dear. Once word got around that my methods were successful with weight loss and body figure maintenance, I made my specialty primarily directed at food addiction and nutrition management."

Her visit was over. They shook hands at his door. "Thank you Dr. Wood...Dr. Potts."

Winnie was about to have dinner when Whitney Zotle, her roommate, spied the big envelope.

"What do you have there Dorf, a new script? Tell me about it." Zotle was a pleasant Type A soul. She worked at a Wall Street satellite office not far from their apartment building. She finished CPA school last year and decided to use her undergrad training in Security Exchange in order to survive financially in New York City.

"No, I went to that doctor I told you about, Dr. Myron Potts. I almost forgot about the info packet." She opened the envelope and out came several pamphlets on things like glycemic index, foods to never eat, foods that make you die, and an eight by ten photo of a large yellow banana. Her thoughts went immediately to her recent confessional. *I must tell dear Father Nesbitt about my vanity and Dr. Potts. Oh, oh, I can't use the word "dear". It now belongs to Dr. Potts.*

Chapter 3
Father Forbish Nesbitt

"I can hear you laughing, Father."

"No one has ever confessed a dream like that to me before, Winnie." He cleared his throat, but it had a giggle sound to it. "Winnie, there must be an explanation."

"Well, about the banana there is. About the sex thing maybe it's because I haven't had a boyfriend for a while."

"I don't understand about the fruit."

"The banana or the boyfriend, Father?"

He started laughing again.

"Father Nesbitt, I'm really concerned about that dream."

"We can't have a discussion here in the confessional. I do have an office. Forgive me if I see humor here, but I can reassure you, even without knowing the details, that your dream is not a sinful or a hell-bound event."

Her heart started to beat fast. "You mean, I can see you in your office?"

"Of course, Winnie, and if you feel uncomfortable about it, we can walk together outside at noon and talk over a hot dog from one of those outside vendors."

Hot dog, that's on the never eat list. "You can have the hot dog, Father. I'll bring a banana."

Again the laughter, I hope he'll understand life according to Dr. Myron Potts

Nesbitt went back to his room at the St. Patrick Parish House. Hearing confessions was always an ambivalent experience for him. While attending priesthood classes he had the feeling the process was an invasion of privacy. Not only that, Nesbitt considered the penance of prayer a meaningless ritual, which released the constituent to go out and commit more sins. It was like giving them permission. With such thoughts Nesbitt experienced a sense of guilt. He had joined the priesthood to feel just the opposite.

The young priest looked at a crucifix with its affixed Jesus on the wall of his spartan room. It was directly across from a wall with a picture of him and his Navy SEAL team. Within the confines of this space he often whispered his thoughts and spoke to the religious icon.

"Religion, even in your times contributed to death and despair amongst the masses." He turned from the cross to the picture of his combat outfit. "Our job was to prevent radical Islamics from killing non-Islamics, like Americans, just because they are just that—non-Islamics. And non-Islamic meant anyone not believing in Allah."

He sat at his student-type desk and removed the silver crucifix around his neck. He spoke to it as if this one also had an effigy of Jesus. "Allah means God. As a Catholic we believe Jesus was more than an emissary or Prophet from God. We believe he is God. Most religions

postulate the existence of God. Buddhism, Judaism, Tao-
ism, Shinto and others also believe in God. So it shouldn't
matter what they call him. For Heaven's sakes, even the
Comanche Indians believe in the Great Spirit who is defined as a God of their understanding. Most of these religions also have some of the same commandments of the
Old Testament…like Confucianism."

Nesbitt jumped to his feet and stood up. He looked
out his only window onto the grassy courtyard. He was
alone. Verbalizing his thoughts like this had almost got him
thrown out of the seminary. "Sometimes Catholicism is
also as narrow-minded of purpose as Islam. Catholicism
preached conversion into its beliefs. Some Islam extremism
mandated conversion or death."

He faced the wall crucifix again. "You died for us.
You are the 'Prince of Peace'." He slammed a fist onto his
desktop. "And I hear violence, bigotry, and hideous sinful
acts at the confessional. I forgive them their actions. I am
not doing what I thought I would be doing by being the
right-hand of God. Collateral death and destruction is oc-
curring sometimes because of religion."

He turned to the closet next to a bureau dresser. *I'm
repeating this scenario almost weekly. Perhaps I should
speak to the Monsignor.* Nesbitt tried turning away from the
closet door. His hand turned the doorknob and he checked
his large Navy duffel bag. It was locked and secure. His
eyes glared at his name stenciled on the side of the bag.

LCDR Forbish Nesbitt USN

"Why do I keep this reminder of what I've done to defend my homeland, its people, and our freedom? Our country was founded on choice of religious beliefs. We don't force our citizens to be Christian, Jewish, or Islamic." He was about to kick the bag in anger but hesitated. *Why injure myself? I should think about positive attributes of living. I should remember that I hear more goodness from our flock rather than their perceived evils.*

Suddenly, a vision of Winifred Dorfinkle appeared as he closed his eyes. He smiled. *She's the only one who seems to be living life and not really objecting. She too seeks answers. There's something electric going on between us—electric or magnetic or both. So much is left unsaid by us because I'm a priest. We've been sending vibrations to each other without transmitting feelings. Well, on my part anyway. I do feel she'll one day outright express her feelings forcing me to reciprocate. For now, I should follow-up on seeing her openly in the prelate advisory offices.*

✦

Winnie placed Father Nesbitt's card next to her cell phone, which meant it was also next to the picture of the banana. This urged her to act now and call him. Father Nesbitt did advise her they should speak at a counseling session. She entered his cellphone number from the card into her personal favorites directory and pressed the send option. He heart beat faster.

I shouldn't be so nervous. He did suggest I talk to him. It was only four days since her confession, and she hesitated. *What would he think if I called him right away? I know what he'd think. He might think I'm suicidal with guilt.* Winnie laughed at the absurdity of the thought. *Who would have suicidal thoughts just because of a sexual dream with a banana?* She'd have to tell him about Dr. Potts or he might just feel that she's just another crazy theatrical student lost in a maze of imagination. She would merely be another actor with an identity crisis. The phone line was ringing.

"Father Nesbitt, here."

"Um…Father…it's me, Winnie…Winifred Dorfinkle."

"Well, hello Winnie. I was just thinking about you."

"You were?" She swallowed and it felt like she sent some vital organ down to her stomach.

"Yes, you know the confessional is primarily a one-way dumping ground. Some people simply externalize actions, thoughts, or ideas, which they consider might be sacrilege."

"Father, I've been thinking a lot about how many ways what I confessed could be taken. But in my mind just having the thought was what I was confessing. I mean, I didn't really do it. Some priests have said in Mass that just thinking about a sin is a sin. You know what I mean?"

He smiled but did not laugh or giggle. "Yes, I know exactly what you mean. The telephone is a good beginning,

Winnie. It signifies a need to go a step further. We should meet as I suggested. I have an office in the small building in back of St. Patrick's."

"Is it private? I mean will anyone else hear us?"

"It's private but with members of the opposite sex we leave the door open."

"I guess these days it's important to do that. I mean with the accusations of priests abusing…" She sucked in a deep breath. "I'm sorry. The stuff in the media is about pedophile and homosexual things. I didn't mean to accuse you of anything. And I definitely will not try to jump your bones." She felt her face getting red and regretted once again that her words came out too fast.

This time Nesbitt could not contain himself. He laughed. "Winnie, Winnie, Winnie, it's okay to talk about such things."

"Well, my dream did have sex in it, sort of. But when I tell you about Dr. Potts, you'll understand." She focused on her fast breathing. She was getting light-headed.

"Doctor? Has a Doctor been taking improprieties with you, Winnie?"

"No, not at all, you're right, we have to talk. Can we meet today? I get out of class at the Thespian at 2:30."

"Okay, but how about 3:30? I'm in room 7. You have to ring the bell to get into the building. Someone will let you in."

"It's a good thing I have no lines to speak in acting class today. I'm so nervous about our meeting."

"Winnie, there's nothing to be nervous about. I'll see you at 3:30." He hung up.

Why do I always put my foot in my mouth? She whispered to the dead phone, "I shouldn't have said anything about the media blitz with sexual abuses and the priesthood. Oh well, I'll just bring the stuff Dr. Potts gave me and see what he thinks. I better not tell him I think he looks like a movie star though." She smiled. "I bet the guy who opens the door is Montague Kelp."

Lying in bed the night of Winnie's confession, Nesbitt's prayers began as he had been taught. "Thank you Jesus for allowing me to help all Catholics." *But why just Catholics? Why not all of God's people? They're all constituents no matter what name they choose to call God—even Allah.*

Sleep came as a sense of falling into a black void. *I've been in this blackness before. I don't want to remember. I don't want the same dream again. But it does happen. It happens every night. I can see it almost like an observer, yet I'm the main player. I can smell it. I wonder if the other survivor has the same rerun over and over again. The other survivor, his name is Omar. Does Omar relive that episode...that evolution into blackness?*

The air in the mosque had changed. The odor of incense and burnt wood persisted ever since Operation Iraqi Freedom. Omar Shahidi finished his Salat prayers. The images of his parents and brother immediately jumped into his head. Thoughts returned of the Americans breaking down their door and asking for his brother, Nabil.

"Which of you is Nabil?" LCDR Nesbitt motioned the four other SEALs to form a circle around the Shahidi family in the dimly lit living room.

Omar spoke the best English and responded. "What do you want with Nabil?"

Nabil, his younger and more athletic brother, immediately pushed one of the SEALs down and headed for the front doorway.

"Wait Nabil. Do not flee. You have done nothing. Wait," Omar shouted.

Nabil replied in Farsi, "They will find my weapons. They will kill us all."

Two of the SEALs grabbed Nabil. Nesbitt took out handcuffs and went to the struggling young Iraqi.

Nabil broke free. He reached into his robe and pulled out a grenade.

"No Nabil. No." Omar rushed forward. A SEAL knocked him unconscious with his rifle.

Omar's parents became agitated. They began reciting Koran scripture as they bent over Omar's body.

The grenade exploded. Everyone in the room was rendered unconscious. Some would never wake up.

Chapter 4

A Walk in the Park

Winnie was having trouble focusing on her classes today. After all, she was about to have a private meeting with Father Nesbitt. Maybe she should take him up on doing the hot dog walk in Central Park versus a St. Patrick office. Her cell phone rang.

"Winnie, this is Father Nesbitt. The office I use is being occupied today and there are no other available spaces. Can we go to Plan B?"

Yes, my God! He read my mind. Or maybe God set this up. "Where will I meet you Father?"

"We can meet at the front of St. Patrick's at 3:30. Central Park entrance is a short block away."

Winnie felt this was a perfect setting. She could unload anything without worrying about being overheard by some stiff-neck traditional Priest or Nun. Some nuns used yard sticks on her in grammar school.

᠊

She was in her last didactic lecture and it was with Professor Bangdot. He was one of the better teachers. *Oh, but my head is still full of Father Forbish Nesbitt. I think Bangdot is looking right at me.*

"For your next assignment, I want each of you to bring something to class."

All eyes stared at him as he leaned forward on the podium. "We all know that many successful actors change their screen names. In my experience, all drama students who seek fame and fortune in the cinematic arts have thoughts about this. And that my dear students is your homework. You will each create a name for yourself as if you are chosen for career-making Hollywood roles."

Winnie wrote the assignment down. Her mind kept sending her to being with Father Nesbitt.

It seems like it took only a few minutes to go from the Thespian classroom to the bronze front doors of St. Patricks. Winnie was early. She stepped into the foyer.

Almost immediately a tall dark figure moved right in front of her causing a sudden fright.

"What do you want? The sanctuary is closed."

The voice was raspy and familiar. He reminded her of the TV monster called the Hulk. As her eyes defined the image as that of Montague Kelp, they both spoke the same words.

"Oh, it's you," Kelp belched out.

"Oh, it's you," Winnie gasped.

"The confessional is closed," Kelp moved in closer.

"I'm waiting for Father Nesbitt." She prayed for Nesbitt's immediate appearance.

"I'm right here Winnie," Nesbitt's voice was like emergency resuscitation.

Kelp rapidly disappeared.

Maybe Kelp's an alien and gets teleported every-where. Her fantasies continued. *I want to jump beside Nes-bitt and cling to his body as if he was going to lift me onto a white horse.*

Nesbitt kept trying to bring up the subject of Dr. Potts as they arrived at Central Park, but Winnie held the conversation on him and his job.

"I bet you like to have breaks in the routine stuff you do, like conducting Mass or Communion."

"Everyone should have breaks from things that be-come ritual in a person's life, Winnie."

They looked at each other and almost got broad-sided by a dog-walker trying to cluster four medium-sized pooches wanting to go in separate directions.

"Well, what do you like best about your job as a priest, Father?" A dog odor lingered.

"I like weddings most. I like the look of expectation of hope, a new life, and commitment."

"Were you ever married or engaged or in a relation-ship before your calling?" Again she seemed to have no control of her words. She had to ask. *After all, he wasn't always a priest.*

"No."

"No what?" She looked at his slight red blush. "Oh, Father, I'm sorry. I mean, I didn't intend to get too person-al." *I did, really.*

"Let's keep our discussion to your confessional. Look there's a Sabrett Hot Dog street cart."

He got two kraut-dogs and two bottles of water, one bottle was for Winnie. She maneuvered their direction to an unoccupied green-slatted park bench.

They looked around and no-one was facing their direction. She started to relax. She felt Central Park was a good venue to contemplate one's troubles—real or imagined. Winnie took her banana from her large handbag along with Dr. Potts' envelope.

"Do you know what a glycemic index of foods is about Father?"

"No."

"Dr. Myron Potts is developing a plan for me to maintain my figure and appearance."

"And he has something to do with bananas and your dream?" Nesbitt thumbed through Potts' tables and held up the large photo of a banana.

"Well, yes. See a banana has a certain glycemic index, which really is the amount of sugar that could be stored as fat if you eat too many. But bananas are in the medium range of sugar content and also have a chemical called dopamine which curbs your appetite." She felt good being a teacher to her dreamy Father Nesbitt.

He started laughing. "So a banana a day keeps the calories away."

"Well, yes but just one. Dr. Potts says to eat a banana a day to cover your twelve awake eating hours. I usually eat mine with breakfast, but I have a lot of schoolwork to do tonight and this banana will carry me through to bed-time."

"I'm beginning to understand. So something hap-pened to stimulate your romance gene and a banana popped into your dream-bank that night."

"Wow, Father, I knew you'd understand." *If he only knew he was the focus of my romantic fantasies.*

Nesbitt swallowed his last bite of hot dog with a long gulp of water and smiled. "It was Sigmund Freud who realized that awake events stimulate the content of our dreams. So Winnie, there's no need to lower your self-im-age by a non-event. Your dream was a mixture of Dr. My-ron Potts banana therapy and normal hormonal stimulation."

It was a relief. *Why didn't I dream of him instead of a banana?* The sunlight was getting warmer. He removed his white collar and all of a sudden he didn't look so priest-like. She had to say something profound or at least non-re-ligious. "You must sweat a lot having to wear black?"

"I think my body is used to black. Most of my Navy uniforms were black."

She tried to segue into his Navy life. "What about camouflage stuff?"

"Black was our camouflage. We mostly worked at night or in the dark."

This conversation is going nowhere. "How often should I...people...go to confession, Father? Do you think I go too much."

"Well, the rule is that if you ask yourself such a question, you should go. However, you should have something to confess first." He wrinkled his brow.

"Mine didn't qualify, huh?" *I feel crestfallen.*

"If you felt it merited coming to St. Patrick's, then it qualifies."

She was no longer crestfallen. *Oh Dear God, what can we talk about now?* "Father, may I ask you a personal question?"

"You already did remember, and I didn't answer it."

"This one's not so nosy." She took a deep breath. "Do you have a Navy tattoo?" *Oh no, another dumb question.*

"Yes," he touched his left sleeve.

"Can I see it?"

"We should be focusing on your confessional."

Her mouth opened and out came, "How did you go from the Navy to a Priest, Father?"

"The military is dedicated to war or using force to keep the peace. As a Priest I'm dedicated only to the teachings of Jesus."

She reddened. Her face felt warm. "Yes, he's the Prince of Peace."

"Let's get back to you. In the two years I've been hearing your confessions there has not been anything blatantly sinful."

"What about dumping my ex-boyfriend Darryl for calling you Father Nebbish?"

"In the Navy a few called me LCDR Nebbish. With a name like Dorfinkle, you should understand about people manipulating names."

"With a name like Nesbitt people don't call you Jewish, do they?" *I wonder where that came from. I'm my own worst enemy.*

"So what if they did. Jesus was called "The Jew" all his life." He smiled. "C'mon lets get some shade. It's too warm in the sun."

They walked another ten minutes. "I never realized how woodsy the Park can be, Father." It seemed like they were the only people on Earth.

"I like to come here when I get too stressed out," Nesbitt looked into Winnie's eyes. "I get to appreciate nature and take a break from looking at skyscrapers and mobs of people always in a hurry."

A voice boomed behind them. "Stop, you two, turn around slowly."

It was a gaunt man in blue jeans, a white-and-blue "peace" logo t-shirt, and sockless low sneakers. He was probably their age. The man brushed some unruly long hair from his left eye. He held a short-barreled revolver pointing at Nesbitt.

"Don't panic or make any noise. I just want your money." He seemed twitchy, jerking his head in all directions while waving the gun.

Father Nesbitt grabbed Winnie's right arm and guided her to his left and slightly behind him. The man's eyes were blinking like he just woke up. "Give me your money. That's all I want. Give it to me and you won't get hurt. You don't want to get killed over money."

Nesbitt's voice was calm yet definitely like someone in charge. "You can put away your weapon right now and walk away fast or stay and face the police."

"What? Are you crazy? I have a gun. Are you blind? One last time...just the money...right now."

"Father, don't." She raised her voice a little—very little. Winnie stared at the mugger. "Don't shoot. He's a priest." She turned to Nesbitt. "Please Father Nesbitt, if he shoots you I'll have to find another confessor." *I'm not a complete nutcase, but I couldn't blurt out my true feelings for him.*

"You can't mess with me. You're just a guy dressed in black." He cocked the hammer. "One last warning or you'll need a priest for last rites for the girl."

Father Nesbitt became a black blur. He moved so fast it was like a click from a camera. His right hand came down on the mugger's gun arm breaking the two forearm bones with a crunch. His extended hand connected sharply with the man's right temple, sending him unconscious to the hard pavement.

"Oh no, Father. Is he dead?" She was so scared she clung to Father Nesbitt with her arms around his waist.

"He'll live. You'll have to let go of me so I can use my cell phone to call the police."

She didn't want to let go. He touched her shoulder and completed his 911 call. The NYPD arrived quickly. They called for an ambulance despite Father Nesbitt's reassurances.

"Don't fret Winnie. He'll only have pain from his broken arm. He'll wake up in an hour."

"How could you do that, Father? You're a priest, and after all we just talked about." Confusion set in because Nesbitt had spoken about peace and Jesus and then just decimated a gun-toting mugger.

"The lesson to be learned, Winnie, is that we are always two people. It will be most important for you, when you're and actress, to leave your make believe world of the theatre and go home to your family in the real world. When this man threatened our mortality, it was time for former LCDR Nesbitt to act, not Father Nesbitt." He put the white plastic collar back onto the shirt. "And you can see all three of us are still alive."

Nesbitt stared at the ceiling in his dark room. *Was my advice to Winnie Dorfinkle really what I believe? Are we all really two people, one for the world to see and a personage for those close to us? I'm a Priest and a Navy SEAL and a person. That's more than two identities. I wonder what life without Winnie to look forward to would be like. Oh dear God, our relationship is supposed to be pure-ly spiritual.*

The blackness of sleep immediately turned to a misty screen as voices without faces visited him yet again. Nesbitt felt stiff. He perceived pain but it was like it belonged to someone else. He heard the same voices continue.

"He's waking up," An Army nurse finished cutting away his combat outfit.

The triage doctor pointed at the other bodies on the floor stretchers. "Any one else alive from that action?"

"He's the only SEAL." The nurse gestured to the gurney next to the Navy SEAL. "This other one is an Iraqi and obviously not the one who triggered the grenade."

"What do we have for IDs?" The Doctor picked through the remains of the black Navy combat uniform.

"We don't know yet about the Iraqi terrorist. This soldier's dogtags says he's LCDR Forbish Nesbitt. The other SEALs are in the morgue unit."

Chapter 5
What's In A Name

Professor Cornish Bangdot stood tall at the podium in front of his drama class. He had just turned fifty and was an established pedagogue of the acting milieu. He had been an actor, screenplay writer, producer, and director. Bangdot dressed like the directors in the early theatre with a beret, shiny silk ascot, riding pants, and polished brown boots.

Winnie sat up front. *I hope today's lecture will help me with my name. I have to wonder though about his name. How could anyone named Cornish Bangdot have ever made it in Hollywood?*

Bangdot leaned on the single-pedestal podium with a riding crop in his right hand. It served as a pointer at the projection screen or at a student. "Today, we are going to discuss the importance of having a correct theatrical name. We've all heard of famous screen and stage stars who in all likelihood would never have been noticed if they struck out on an entertainment career with their birth names. Cary Grant was in reality Archibald Leach. John Wayne was born Marion Morrison." He stared at Winnie's's grin.

"Yes, I know what Winnie here and some of you are thinking. What about my name? Cornish Bangdot, indeed. Why didn't I change it? The truth be known is that to change my name would bring about a disinheritance from the noble and wealthy Bangdot family. However, I feel my destiny is to be here today to teach and to train promising theatricals like you." Bangdot slapped the riding crop against his right leg producing a sharp "snap". "So, this morning your assignment was to pick out a name and tell the class why it was chosen. We'll start with a man first and then a lady and continue to alternate the genders." He pointed the crop at a red-haired young man three rows down.

The student stood and placed both hands onto the back of his chair. "I have red hair and my first thoughts were to emulate stars like Red Skelton and Red Buttons. The name I picked, however, is one that has history like Jason of the Argonauts. The last name of Clancy to me, conjures up the mighty tomes of literature by the military thriller author, Tom Clancy. At this point in my career, I favor adventure, thriller, romance, and drama roles. My given name of Jason Clancy seems like a macho choice."

The entire class laughed. Bangdot smiled. "Some successful actors and actresses have in fact kept their birth names. I think your choice to keep your real name for those reasons is a wise one." He turned to the front row. "Let's take a young lady next. Winifred, I'm eager to hear how you managed today's exercise."

She swallowed hard and stood beside her chair. "I've given this a lot of thought." Winnie turned from the Professor to the rest of the class. "I believe a professional celebrity cultivate both a theatrical name and keep their birth name when they go home from work. My name is

Winifred Dorfinkle. My first name could be mistaken for a man's name so I will change that. My last name, well it's been the butt of many jokes and manipulations from 'Fink', 'Dork', 'Tinkle' and , from our family parrot Claudia,' just plain 'Finkle'." She waited for the laughter to stop. "I choose a name which can span comedy, romance, action, crime drama, memoirs, and athletics. My stage name will be Rebecca Winslow." Her immediate thought was to have Father Nesbitt's opinion. She could hardly wait for their next meeting.

Nesbitt sat at his student desk looking at his laptop email page. It was from the NYPD. He read the email aloud, "Father Nesbitt, please come to armed robbery detective Norman Bauman's office at NYPD Central Building & Police Plaza at 4PM tomorrow. If this is inconvenient please give us some alternative times. If you cannot comply Lt. Bauman will arrive between 9AM and 5PM at St. Patrick's. If you are not available a warrant will be issued and you will be brought in for more detailed questioning regarding your story about the 'attempted armed robbery' in Central Park yesterday. Please note, the perpetrator claims you assaulted him, breaking his right forearm, and inflicting head trauma causing a possible concussion. He is also talking of suing the Catholic Church for unprovoked assault and battery."

Nesbitt stroked his large crucifix and fingered its chain. "Dear Jesus, the finger of persecution still falls on one who professes peace and tranquility."

⋇

"So how did it go, Rebecca Winslow?" Whitney Zotle smiled as Winnie entered their apartment.

"Well, Professor Bangdot said it met the qualifications of being a celebrity name allowing for proper development of a brand." Dorfinkle dropped her backpack on her bed and sat next to it.

"Brand?"

"Yes, he said theatrical stars need a name which can lend itself to easy flow off the tongue. The name must be able to have familiar offshoots. Rebecca can easily become 'Becky' which is a nickname that has identification potential. Like 'Liz' means Elizabeth Taylor."

"You could've kept Winifred. 'Winnie has good brand potential." Zotle grinned.

"I thought of that roomy, but Professor Bangdot said that with my last name as Dorfinkle there would be a good chance that the media would focus on it. I mean, like Archibald Leach would have ruined Cary Grant's career if he kept either the 'Archibald' or the 'Leach.'"

They both laughed. Zotle held up a newspaper. "I see you and your Priest didn't make much of a splash with your robbery. It only rated two-sentences in the police report section. There was no mention of either your name or Father Nesbitt."

"Yeah, it's probably for the best. The church doesn't advocate violence, you know. Father Nesbitt could get a reprimand." She shook off her loafers as her cell phone ringtone produced Tarzan's call of the apes.

Winnie stared wide-eyed at the caller ID. "Oh my God! It's the NYPD."

Half-way around the world, a once peace-minded Iraqi was also thinking of Forbish Nesbitt. Omar Shahidi was brought back to his home after investigation and interrogation confirmed that his brother Nabil, and not he, Omar, had terrorist ties to Al Qaeda. Autopsy evaluation of his dead parents and sibling confirmed that Nabil was the one who detonated the explosive device.

Shahidi looked around the combination living and eating room. Black char had replaced the soft tan wall coloring. The furniture lay in its terminal state of burnt cloth and splintered wood. His bitterness at the Americans was enhanced by their refusal to allow his Salat prayers while he was in their custody. He took out the letter of exoneration he received at his discharge. He read aloud the one part that had become a loop of words which seemed to play spontaneously when he thought about the Navy SEALs' invasion into his home.

"This letter will let it be known that Omar Shahidi has been found not to have ties with Al Qaeda. That his bother, Nabil Shahidi, was responsible for triggering an explosive device resulting in his death and the deaths of his parents and three American soldiers." It was signed by the Commanding Officer of the local Marine detachment and by a Navy SEAL—LCDR Forbish Nesbitt.

Shahidi pulled back the curtains on the right wall letting in the bright sun. He found a serviceable stool and sat on it while watching dust swirl in the light rays as the minimal breeze entered the open doorway. He looked back at the letter and spoke to the felt presence of his deceased family. "I know that name, Nesbitt. I heard several times that Nesbitt was the other survivor and leader of the SEAL patrol that killed my loved ones."

He focused on one sentence,...*three American soldiers.* "My three family members were killed and Allah took three Americans. It is just and written." He read it aloud again.

Suddenly a dark shadow filled the doorway. A voice flowed in with an air of authority. "Three for three is not retribution. There is one left. Vengeance must be done and the world must know of it." The dark shadow became a dark-robed man with an AK-47 slung over his right shoulder. "Nabil and your mother and father are in Paradise now, but will not rest until you destroy the leader of the destruction of all that you and Allah held dear."

Shahidi recognized the face as that of a friend of Nabil's. The man was known only as Nahlid, an Al Qaeda unit commander. "I know the looks and name of that leader. His name is Nesbitt. If he had never come to Iraq, none of this would have happened."

"Allah has destined that you survived to punish the evil American whose intrusion into your sanctified house led to this devastation." Nahlid placed a toughened, scarred hand on Shahidi's shoulder.

Chapter 6
Debriefing

Nesbitt was told to wait outside the Monsignor's office. His thoughts drifted back to his last Navy SEAL Iraqi action and recovery from his wounds. Lately he'd been questioning whether his priesthood had been a true calling. Nesbitt allowed reminiscence of the past that led to his career change from Navy SEAL to Catholic Priest. He had two primary Navy doctors. One was a surgeon who repaired his external injuries together with a plastic surgeon. His main problem now, he knew, was his PTSD. He needed help with his mind. The action in Iraq that resulted in the deaths of three of his team, and all but one of an Iraqi family, haunted him.

"Your body heals well, LCDR Nesbitt. The fact that you remember everything in detail negates any permanent damage from a cerebral concussion." Experienced PTSD Navy psychiatrist, Primo Corella, read the nursing notes in his chart. "You're still having flashbacks in the form of nightmares according to the night-shift nurses."

Nesbitt shifted in his chair and straightened his-white work uniform. The short-sleeve shirt had an open collar, but he still felt warmer than the ambient temperature warranted. "Dr. Corella, as a soldier I deal with the Islamic extremists as enemies of our country." He swallowed and took a deep breath. "My job as a combatant is to destroy the enemy." He readjusted his crossed knees. "Do you know what the terrorists call us? I'll tell you. They don't refer to US soldiers as their enemy. They call us infidels, unbelievers, blasphemers against Allah and the Koran. They fight for the God of their understanding."

Corella leaned forward, "Are you saying their actions do not have military objectives?"

"I'm saying that their actions are driven by belief in their God. The Jihadists, who are not in military uniform, are against our democratic, liberal, and capitalistic lifestyle. They don't mind dying in Allah's name. It's a direct ticket to Paradise–their idea of Heaven."

"LCDR Nesbitt, you talk of terrorists, organized military extremists like the Al Qaeda, and their Jihad. And yes, they are taught that this is a holy war. But Forbish, the extremists are called that because other Islamics do not believe in such a bloody quest for promoting their Faith. The extremists represent only 2% of the Muslim world. The rest are peaceable, well-meaning people. The first book of the Koran reflects that. It even recognizes Jesus as advocating peaceable coexistence."

Nesbitt wiped sweat from his forehead with a square-folded handkerchief. "I understand that, and I also understand that Hitler started out with only 2% and mesmerized the masses into what became World War II." He looked down and then up again. "Dr. Corella, I can no longer be a combat soldier. It seems to me like we're killing the equivalent of churchgoers."

Corella sat back creaking the spring in his desk chair. "I see from your file that you've become an avid church attendee."

"It's become an obsession. Jesus was the Prince of Peace. I'm a Catholic. I left the church when I read about the history of the Popes who instigated wars like the Crusades. Wars based on targeting religions of others."

"Now you're back again, Forbish. Why? Why are you now embracing Christianity?"

"I don't know. When I talked with the Catholic Chaplin, he said I might be experiencing a calling. I've been thinking a lot lately about that…about becoming a priest."

⸺

"You can go in now, Father," Monsignor Hannon's secretary broke Nesbitt's reverie and opened the Monsignor's door. Nesbitt had received the expected summons to the Monsignor's office with some anxiety. He fingered his black rosary beads as he entered the dimly lit room with book-covered walls. The tomes seemed organized by size and color. Hannon raised his head from his computer keyboard.

"Please sit down in front of me, Father Nesbitt." His tone lacked any threat.

"Yes, Monsignor." Nesbitt sat back in the blue brocade, parlor-like chair facing the dark mahogany desk.

"You were right in telling me last evening about yesterday's issue in Central Park. As I told you, the event should never have happened." Monsignor Hannon raised his palm to defray any interruption. "There's a reason we have offices here at St. Patrick. If your visit to discuss a confessional matter, or any matter, had been done here, the criminal confrontation would not have occurred." He folded his hands. "And the police involvement would also have been a non-event. The police, by the way, were very courteous about contacting my office. They cc'd me on their email to you."

"Sir, the church sanctions home visits, discussions with various church groups, and even outdoor events to do benedictions and such. My one-on-one with Winifred Dorfinkle, involved a confessional excerpt, which I felt needed a more relaxed environment for our constituent. And it was...until the man with the gun appeared."

"Have you made your appointment with Detective Bauman?"

"Yes, it's today here in office seven at the St. Patrick Annex."

"Very good, it's my hope there won't be any press involvement. Reporters must get permission from the Cardinal to enter our sanctuary for business purposes. They often, however, wait like vultures on our street-side stairs."

"Sir, the mugger must have a criminal record. I've been a citizen in good standing, and my military record is exemplary."

"Look at it from the press's point of view. You're a Navy SEAL in a priest's frock using your combat skills against a man allegedly just walking in Central Park. Even now you often call me 'Sir' instead of Monsignor." Hannon's face reddened slightly. "The media love anything slanderous or scandalous relative to the Church, the military, Central Park, or especially New York City." He stood up. "Let's face it. They'll play up the fact that you went against a man with a gun and used your SEAL training to overpower him, break his arm, and render him unconscious."

"But Monsignor, he could have used the gun on both of us. He threatened us."

"Be realistic, Forbish. The only way this could play right for us, would be if the gunman was an ex-convict or has a criminal record including murder, extortion, armed robbery, and KKK membership." He sipped from his teacup. "Has the woman, this Dorfberg, also been contacted by the NYPD?"

"It's Dorfinkle, and the answer is yes."

"How do you know?"

"She called me and emailed me. Her story will be exactly like mine because it's the truth…it's what happened"

"The media won't care. If they can sell papers or get the TV news to run with it, they'll present both sides and leave it for the public to decide. In the meantime, there will be a news blitz that could threaten your's and my job." Hannon walked Nesbitt to the door. "The Cardinal has advised that you stick to your priestly vocation in answer to all queries. Do not give out any anecdotes or Navy SEAL war tidbits. Say as little as possible. And even with that, the risk of you being misquoted is close to 100%." Hannon put a hand on Nesbitt's shoulder. "Have you cleared this detective for entry into St. Patrick's?"

"Absolutely, Montague Kelp is skulking around now waiting for him. He'll bring him, and only him, directly to office number seven."

Nesbitt looked at his watch. He had two hours before noon, before Detective Norman Bauman appeared. He went to his room and removed his cell phone from its charger, scrolled his phone's few contacts, and pressed *Dorfinkle.*

"Hello, Winnie's phone."

"Winnie, it's Father Nesbitt."

"I'm glad you called. I meet with Lt Bauman at two o'clock at Police Plaza."

"Police Plaza? That's kind of intimidating, isn't it? Couldn't you find a coffee shop or public place with people around?"

"Oh, I'm sure I'll feel safe there. Actually, I could use the experience for a play we'll be doing in the spring. Father, we didn't get a chance to talk about anything other than describing just what happened in the park. Are you in trouble with the church?"

"Could be. St. Patrick's is worried that the press might slant everything against us and not the mugger."

"How could they?"

"Let's face it. That's what they do. If you get any calls from the National Informer hang up right away. Look, what I called about was the confessional. Everything heard in the confessional is privileged and confidential information. I will never disclose what you presented and why we took the walk in Central Park other than we were discussing church protocol."

"So I shouldn't tell the police or anyone about my dream, Dr. Potts, or the banana?"

"Winnie, if you publicly declare what you told a Priest in confession, it could have disastrous effects on the church. It would mean to millions of Catholics, that what they say in confidence to a Priest could become media fodder."

"Oh, no, no, I'll tell only about the crook with the gun and what he said."

"Okay, call me tonight after we're both done with our police interviews." Nesbitt disconnected. *I have bad feelings about this.*

✦

Over two thousand miles away, Omar Shahidi paced his dusty floor with conflicted thoughts. There was no wind and the inside of Shahidi's home was still oppressively hot in the mid-afternoon sun. He sat on a straw-stuffed cushion in the shade offered by the overhanging roof. The shade was still hot but the inside of his home was hotter. It had been weeks since his first meeting with Nahlid who directed Shahidi to meet others like him who had not been Jihad sympathizers until disaster or hardship came to them via US military action. The frequent meetings also solidified his faith in Islam. Innocent Muslims were the oppressed. The oppressors had occupied his country. The oppressors were Americans. *One American above all others must be killed.* Nahlid was coming today to discuss how this might be possible.

Chapter 7
Omar Shahidi

Shahidi arranged another straw-stuffed futon across from him beneath the shaded overhang of his stone-walled house. He greeted Nahlid with salutations acknowledging Allah as blessing their meeting.

"Salam-u-Alaikum (peace be unto you)," Nahlid offered.

"Wa-Alaikumussalam wa-Rahmatullah, (may the peace, mercy, and blessings of Allah be upon you)." Shahidi waved his right hand with the words.

Black-robed Nahlid's extra inches of height over Shahidi were nullified as he sat looking across from him. Shahidi's white robe had a few sand-colored stains from his frequent house-cleaning chores. Nahlid nodded approval of Shahidi clutching his weathered version of the Koran. He stroked his salt-and-pepper beard and pointed to the holy book as he spoke, "Omar, it is good you seek solace in the wisdom of the book of Allah."

"My brother died for the one true God. He died as a soldier of Allah killing three infidels as he went to Paradise." Shahidi tightened his grip on the book.

"You have been to many meetings these past months. I have seen you. Others who have spoken with you tell of your heightened faith in Mohammad's teachings and Allah's words."

"Nahlid, I have come to believe that I survived to continue my brother Nabil's work against the unbelievers who have invaded our land." He put both hands on the Koran and raised it in front of him. "I must avenge my father, mother, and brother. I must become part of our Jihad."

"We think you are ready to progress from philosophy of purpose into action. Can you leave your business two days a week for physical training?" Nahlid moved his crude futon closer to Shahidi. "You will be trained for such a mission. Unlike a soldier in the ranks of many men and women, you are destined for seeking out this Navy SEAL Nesbitt and destroying him."

"Am I to sacrifice myself like my brother in this process?" Shahidi did not sound fearful.

"No, Omar, you are to become an outwardly peaceable Islamic, who will find himself comfortable living with and mingling with the infidels."

Shahidi sat up straight, "Living with them?"

"You're English is too accented right now. You must learn their ways, their habits, and speak their tongue with great acuity. You are to blend in with them in their land."

"But Nahlid, how will I find the Navy Nesbitt–the killer of my family." Shahidi stood up.

"We will find him. When your training is judged complete, we will send you to where this Nesbitt can be found."

Shahidi paced the small patio, "He is military. How can I get close to him without my true purpose being discovered?"

"Nesbitt has been injured. This we know. He will be sent back to his homeland and either remain in a combat unit or given a non-tactical assignment in America. It is also possible Nesbitt will leave the Navy because of his injuries or by choice." Nahlid produced a small folded paper from inside his black robe. "We have informants within the US military. We will track Nesbitt while you are becoming a soldier of Allah."

Shahidi stopped the slow circular movements, "What if he is no longer in the military?"

Nahlid stood close and placed a hand on Shahidi's shoulder, "We will then wait until taking him out will also include many other infidels."

"And I can do this without self-sacrifice?" Shahidi's eyes widened with the query.

"You will understand how to do this with your training." Nahlid embraced Shahidi. "You are to begin in three days."

They parted with raised right hands.

Nahlid initiated the words, "Maʿ al-salāmah" (with peace).

" Fī amān Allāh" (In Allah's protection), Shahidi replied."

Shahidi watched his mentor's dark form disappear like a shadow coming into sunlight. His feelings were mixed at his now defined role of not only an avenger but as a true member of an Al Qaeda Jihad. He was now part of the Holy War against the United States.

Detective Lt. Norman Bauman was startled by the Quasimodo-like sudden appearance of the bulky Montague Kelp.

"Who are you? What do you want? You must have an appointment to go to the annex buildings." Kelp's bass voice seemed to send out palpable vibrations along with the words.

"What? I'm NYPD Detective Lieutenant Bauman— here to see Father Forbish Nesbitt." Bauman flashed his ID at his amorphous greeter who stepped back into the shadows away from the sudden thrust of the leather-cased credentials.

"You must follow me." Kelp shuffled forward not looking back at Bauman. His rag-like clothing made flag-flapping sounds.

Bauman looked around as he followed his unusual receptionist.

Kelp came to a sudden stop and pointed with an outstretched tattered-sleeved arm at the single story Annex. "Room number 7," he rasped.

Bauman looked at the door number and turned to thank the man but he had already disappeared. Bauman knocked on the door.

"Come in please. It's not locked." Nesbitt's tones were friendly.

Bauman looked around the room as his eyes adjusted to the dim light.

Nesbitt pointed to a wicker-woven chair to the right of the small dark wood table which was the only other furniture item in the spartan room.

Bauman presented his ID and looked at the crucifix above Nesbitt.

Nesbitt smiled, "He's always with us, Detective."

Bauman looked around expecting to see someone else in the windowless chamber.

"Jesus…Jesus is always with us. The cross with his effigy is a mere reminder."

"Yes, well, let me formally introduce myself." He flashed the picture-badge ID. "I'm Detective Norman Bauman, NYPD."

"I recognize you from the Times picture covering the Central Park incident."

"Father, I'm emphasizing the importance of my credentials. There are people in this city who call themselves journalists. Some are proper newspeople but a few, and they are always perched like vultures when they sense a news item can be transformed into sensationalism, may misrepresent themselves as being from the NYPD. Do you understand my implication, Father."

Nesbitt, sat forward, "Of course, even our Monsignor has briefed all of us at St. Patricks to be wary of who we see and what we say."

Bauman crossed his knees, "Good, I've read your statement from the uniformed officer at the crime scene. I have it with me. However, and this is just routine police work Father, will you please tell me in your own words what happened yesterday?"

"Yes, Detective, I was walking with Ms. Winifred Dorfinkle in Central Park. We were discussing a church matter when a young man with a gun came upon us suddenly and demanded money."

"Is that all he said?"

"When I hesitated, he then added that he would kill us if we didn't empty our wallets immediately. Then he cocked the gun."

"What kind of gun was it, Father?"

"A loaded two-inch Colt .38 Special Revolver. The NYPD officer retrieved it at the scene."

"You could tell that it was loaded? How is it that you're familiar with firearms, Father?"

Nesbitt gave Bauman and icy stare. "Lieutenant Bauman, you know very well I, like many other American citizens, have served in the military at some point in our lives."

"Yes, forgive me Father, you were in the Navy I understand."

"Were you ever in the service Lieutenant?"

"Yes, also the Navy," Bauman smiled. "I apologize Father, but let me be upfront. The press will come right out and portray you as a former Navy SEAL and a trained killer."

"Those may be their words. I plan not to talk about my military service." Nesbitt folded his muscular arms. "As I do now, Detective."

"Okay, Father, what action by the alleged mugger prompted you to defend yourself and disarm the man."

"He tightened his finger around the trigger with the gun fully loaded and cocked the hammer. The Colt snub nose at the cocked position goes from a six-pound trigger pull to less than two pounds of pressure to fire it. He was about to shoot Ms. Dorfinkle."

"Ms. Dorfinkle?"

"He moved his aim from me to her and was squeezing the trigger. It was the only chance I had to prevent her from being shot. I deflected his gun arm downward and hit him in the side of his head with my fist. The man fell to the ground unconscious without firing the weapon. And that, Lieutenant Bauman is what happened."

"I believe you, Father, and I strongly advise you to never deviate from using the exact language you've just used whenever you have to repeat the sequence of events."

"Then why are you here?"

"I'm here to listen to what you're saying to counter the mugger's attempt to reverse the scenario. All criminals try to point the finger of blame away from themselves. This one is not only doing it, he's attempting to extort money from the church and get paid by any news-rag that publishes slander and accusatory outlandish situations."

Nesbitt folded his hands on the table. "The church has not been approached to my knowledge. I also haven't heard or seen anything in the TV news."

"As far as the church goes that's a 'not-yet' event. As for the newspapers, I can tell you truthfully that the NYPD has had over a dozen queries from the likes of supermarket checkout rags similar to *The Informer, Lawsuit, Confidential,* and *The Un-American.* They have reporters camped outside the steps of St. Patricks who I'm sure will approach me as soon as I leave here."

"And what do you say to them, Lieutenant?"

"I keep it simple. I just use two words–'No Comment.'"

"Have you done background checks on me and Ms. Dorfinkle?"

"Father, such things are automatic with the police. You're both model citizens, although…" Bauman stopped.

"Although what?"

"Most of your Navy SEAL operations and training are secret stuff. The Navy is not releasing anything."

"Okay, Detective, what about the gunman. How pristine is he?"

"Father, he's been in trouble since he was nine-years old. He's been in juvenile court, jail, and his adult life is measured by eleven arrests for assault, battery, theft, and aggravated robbery. Aggravated means he used a weapon. This is in fact the third time for him with attempted armed robbery, which is an automatic life in prison plus five more for a second offense with carrying a firearm. This guy is screaming he's innocent, that it wasn't his gun, and that of course you two were mugging him."

"What about fingerprints on the gun?"

"They're all his. He claims you wiped your prints off and put the gun in his hand after you knocked him out." Bauman raised both arms in frustration. "In this country, you're innocent until proven guilty. His lawyer will be out to prove his innocence."

"There's no way that can happen. There was no one else there but us."

"You didn't hear me, Father. His lawyer will plead his case by any means. I know him, he's as sleazy as Malcom."

"Malcom?"

"The perpetrator's name, Father, is Malcom Flenk. His lawyer, Rodney Ducette, will be getting money from the street papers as he feeds them sensational misinformation about you and the girl."

Chapter 8
Winifred Dorfinkle

"Look out the window, Dorf." Zotle lifted one slat on the venetian blind.

"Wow, where did those people come from?"

"There's a TV camera truck parked half on the sidewalk. You can bet they're all media hounds waiting to pounce on you."

"What am I goin to do? I have to meet that Detective at Police Plaza."

"Not to worry, roomy. I have a plan."

"A plan? Like what?"

"It's simple. I'll need your Drama Academy hoodie. I won't need anything else."

"It's quarter to one. I'm leaving now. I want to give myself plenty of time to get there."

Zotle pulled the Drama college logo sweater over her head and adjusted it's slightly snug fit. "Okay, Dorf, I go out the back entrance. Give me five minutes and then you go out the front."

"I go out the front? They'll smother me."

"No, they won't, Dorf dear. There are a dozen reporters covering the rear entrance. When they see me they'll alert the front journalist mob. Believe me I have to arrange press conferences at Wall Street . I know how to do this."

"Do you think I'm dressed okay for the Police interview?" Winnie twirled around. She wore a light blue sweater and a knee-length dark blue skirt. Beneath the skirt black leggings disappeared into white sneakers.

"The white shoes stand out like a bullseye target. Put your black Crocs on."

Winnie complied. "I meant about my outfit. Do I look okay for my interview with the Detective?"

"Yes...without the white Nikes. Anything is okay for the Police. I mean this isn't for a job interview, you know."

They both laughed. Winnie looked at her Micky Mouse watch. "We better get started."

Zotle opened the rear entry door, took one step outside and feigned shock at the small group with cellphone and regular cameras at the ready. She immediately slammed the door closed and went back into the building. The press reps neared the door all shouting at once. Their numbers suddenly increased as the larger group from the front entrance swarmed to merge with their smaller numbers.

They shouted simultaneously, "Winifred! Dorfinkle! Miss Dorfinkle! Ms. Dorfinkle!"

Zotle pulled the hoodie forward shading her fore-head and eyes. She cracked open the door and pleaded, "Please, I have to leave. I have a class to attend."

A reporter managed to get his toe wedged in the door and another pulled it open. A third gabbed Zotle by the arm. "What's your story Winifred? Did you and the Priest really assault that man in Central Park."

Zotle pushed a path to gain access to a side street around the apartment building. She offered only one word, "No." Her main body tactic for crowd-penetration was to keep turning around like a ballet dancer. It always worked at Wall Street Press crowds and it was working now.

As soon as the crowd dissipated from the building's front entrance, Winnie dashed out the front and ran across the street. She disappeared quickly down the subway station staircase one block away. No one followed her. By the time she arrived at her stop at Pearl Street for 1 Police Plaza, her pulse and breathing had normalized.

Detective Norman Bauman was located on the fourth floor. A receptionist called ahead to alert Bauman to Winnie's presence. He was waiting for her across from the elevator .

"Ms. Dorfinkle?" Bauman motioned her forward with a wave of his arm.

Winnie was all eyes, taking in the crowded visage of cubicles, side-by-side desks, and the three walled-in rooms with stenciled detectives names on the opaque glass windowed doors. "Yes, you're Detective Bauman?"

"Yes, please come with me. I'm in the last office to the right."

Bauman had her sit directly across from him. He sat with a straight back in his maroon cracked-leather chair.

Winnie looked around the partly cluttered room. The only sounds were distant intermittent muted voices of the cube and open-air occupants. She sat with her hands on her lap at the junction of her jacket and leggings. She said nothing as advised by Father Nesbitt.

Bauman opened a small memo notebook and spoke, "You are Ms. Winifred Dorfinkle? The young woman who was with Father Forbish Nesbitt in Central park yesterday?"

"Yes, officer." Her voice was soft as she tried for a sympathetic victim-like countenance.

"You can call me Detective. What shall I call you?"

"Most people call me Winnie. And Yes Detective, I was with Father Nesbitt yesterday."

"Well, Winnie, the purpose of today's meeting is to ascertain what took place at that Central Park encounter." He clicked his generic ballpoint twice. "Before I ask you any questions, I want you to tell me what happened." He motioned her to begin.

"I had made an appointment to discuss a church matter with Father Nesbitt. It was such a nice day, we decided to have our meeting in the Park. We talked back-and-forth and had lunch from one of those hot dog vendors." Winnie took a deep breath and tried to clear her dry throat.

Bauman reached around to a small refrigerator behind him and gave her a small bottle of cold spring water. "Your mouth must be dry. It happens to everyone. Being interviewed by the police does that, especially to innocent citizens."

Winnie tried to swallow but couldn't. She accepted the water. "Really, I mean guilty people don't get nervous or afraid?"

"On the contrary, most come across as angry at the police and insulted that they're here."

She gulped two swigs, "How about the guy who was going to shoot us? Was he mad like that?"

Bauman smiled, "He was outraged, not only at being here, but being here in handcuffs and locked up in a cell. Can you please go on with your story, Winnie?"

"Okay, Detective, after we finished eating, we began walking away from all the park benches and the people. We were actually almost finished our talk when this man jumped at us from a clump of bushes next to a large tree. He had a gun. He demanded our money or he would kill us." Winnie put her hands to her chest, "Me first and then he'd shoot Father Nesbitt. I mean, he pointed the gun at Father Nesbitt first and after Father Nesbitt tried reasoning with him, he turned the gun on me."

"What happened next?"

"Detective, it was awful, the man said he'd shoot me first and then kill the Father. He said he'd just soon as take the money from our bodies if we didn't hand it to him. He looked at Father Nesbitt and then back to me. That's when Father Nesbitt grabbed for the gun and hit the man's gun arm. The man attacked Father Nesbitt but the Father hit him and the man fell to the asphalt walkway. He was unconscious."

Bauman finished his writing after a minute of silence and sat back. "Okay, this is the part where I ask questions. First, this man with the gun, had you ever met him before?"

"No, Detective."

"You said he appeared from the foliage. Was he not casually walking and you confronted him?"

"No, Detective,"

"You said he had a gun in his hand. Were you or Father Nesbitt carrying a gun?"

"No, Detective."

"Did the man introduce himself to you at any time?"

"No Detective."

"Did Father Nesbitt at any time warn the man that he would hurt him and demand that he, the man with the gun must give him, and you, all his money?"

"No, Detective." Suddenly Winnie started laughing. She saw the puzzled look in Bauman's face. "I'm sorry, Detective. I'm a drama student and our conversation is most unstimulating on my part. I keep saying 'no Detective'. I've never seen a screenplay or stage play script where the victim only says two words to the police."

"Okay, Winnie. At this point I have to tell you what this gunman told us, the police, when he regained consciousness. This man, Malcom Flenk...."

Winnie began laughing again. "Malcom Flenk? That's his name." She laughed again.

"Why is that so funny?" Bauman folded his hands.

"Flenk? I mean he must be related to Montague Kelp." She started laughing louder. "Probably cousins, Malcom Flenk...and...Montague Kelp, of the New York City Flenks and Kelps."

"You've got me laughing and I don't why, Winnie." Bauman smiled.

Winnie explained about Kelp and how names are important in the theatre.

"Winnie, please let me finish my sentence about Mr. Flenk. When he came to, he told us he was taking a leisurely walk through Central Park when you and Father Nesbitt approached him. Flenk said....Winnie please don't laugh. Flenk said that you said hello to him and that Father Nesbitt then pulled the gun on him and demanded his wallet."

Winnie took a deep breath. "No Detective, it happened like I said. Oh, wait a minute, you said he said Father Nesbitt...used his name...knew he was a Priest?"

"Yes, he said you and the Priest accosted him."

"Wrong…wrong…wrong, Detective. Father Nesbitt took his white plastic collar off because of the heat, long before Flenk appeared from the bushes. I was the one who told Flenk to stop his mugging because Father Nesbitt was a Priest and we didn't have any money."

"What happened after you said that?"

"That's when he said he'd shoot us dead if we didn't give him our cash."

Bauman made Winnie repeat her statement two more times. "Winnie, I'm going to write up our meeting of today and prepare it for you to read and sign as being the words used here. I'll need you to come back, or I can meet you at a place where someone can witness your signature."

"No, it's better I come here. My witnesses would be my fellow students and that would be very awkward for me."

"Okay, can we meet again tomorrow around lunch, here in my office?"

"Yes, Detective."

"Wow, you finally said 'Yes, Detective'." He smiled and escorted her to the elevator. He extended his hand as a departure gesture and then burst out laughing

"Detective, what's so funny?"

"I just remembered. I met Montague Kelp earlier when I interviewed Father Nesbitt. You're right, their names seemed to suit them. They could be cousins."

Chapter 9
The Tutorial

Nurse Gertrude Pickles faced the tutorial class. "Ordinarily this class of first-time patients is so small that we include you with the students in the one-year treatment group. However, Dr. Potts' practice is growing faster than anticipated. We try to keep the classroom size to less than twenty individuals. Any more and the group becomes an audience rather than an effective student body."

Dr. Myron Potts entered the small room. A six-foot square screen was centered to receive slides from a ceiling PowerPoint projector. "Good evening, class. It's most important now to start your journey into the world of correct eating." He unbuttoned his long white lab coat. "Our biggest enemy is sugar. Sugar is usually thought of in terms of table sugar or sucrose. And, as this slide shows, it's not really the sucrose itself, but what comprises the sucrose molecule." He pointed a red laser dot onto the screen which was the signal for Pickles to change the image.

"As you can see, sucrose is made up of two molecules of glucose. Now let's look at other sugars." A new image appeared, "These are also sugars: maltose, lactose, and fructose. These have one molecule of our foe—glucose. You will also see and hear about sugar alcohols. These are merely chemical additions of a hydroxyl group and still contain one molecule of glucose. Some of the deadly sugar alcohols are called sucralose, sorbitol, lactitol, and maltitol." He paused and shut his laser pointer off. Winnie raised her hand.

"Yes, we have a question from our newest member. Please introduce yourself to the group."

"I'm Winifred, Winnie, Dorfinkle. May I ask why these sugars and sugar alcohols are what you call deadly?"

Potts was all smiles and rubbed his hands together. "Oh yes my dear, that is a wonderful and an appropriate question. The answer lies in the next few slides." He signaled Pickles.

"This slide shows what we call labelling. From this point on in your life, you must read and be familiar with the ingredients of all foodstuffs you buy, especially the ones you eat." Potts pointed his red dot at a label on the packaging of a popular brand of ice cream. "Sugar free it says. Look at the ingredient makeup and what do we see." He pointed to a woman in the middle row seat. "Please read it to us my dear."

The overweight lady stood, "I'm Drazella Little. The words are 'Sugar Free'."

Potts did a pirouette turning a complete circle. His white lab coat flapped open. "Yes, yes, yes, you see. The label lies. This ice cream contains both lactose and lactitol. Two types of sugars. Not only that, too much of the sugar alcohols will produce diarrhea. Let's have the next slide." A box of diet cookies flashed on the screen. "Same label here…Sugar Free. And it's mostly sucralose and maltitol.

Lies again. Remember these molecules release one molecule of glucose, our deadly enemy. Whenever you see a label of sugar alcohols with a number after it, simply divide by two and thats' the amount for free sugar or glucose. In this case the number is 12, so the free glucose content will be six. Thus, my dear people, it's true there's no sugar, ie no sucrose, but definitely there is our villain…glucose."

Nurse Pickles distributed handouts of pages of foods advertised as containing no sugar and being the same misrepresentation as the others.

Potts walked up and down the aisle and back to the screen. "Your lifetime job is to read nutrition data. You must read labels."

Gertrude Pickles took the podium at the end of Dr. Potts one hour presentation of "Glucose, hidden in plain sight." She addressed the class. "Next session will be even more enlightening. Dr. Potts will reveal the not so mysterious Glycemic Index of foods."

Winnie felt uplifted. *Dr. Potts is backing up his theories with fact. So far this is getting to be worthwhile.* Her cellphone vibrated with an appointment announcement. It was a reminder of her meeting with Lieutenant Bauman at noon tomorrow.

Omar Shahidi also attended classes. He also learned new words. He learned to speak slow English and pronounce certain alphabetic letters correctly. It was discouraging at first. Nahlid served as his mentor.

"Speak slowly isolating each syllable of the American English words. The more you speak like an American, the more believable you'll be that you have lived in the United States many years. You must distance yourself from having lived in Iraq."

"I wish to complete my language training as fast as possible. I must be able to face Nesbitt while I end his life." Shahidi lapsed into a rapid delivery.

"You see what just happened? You talk of revenge, you get angry, you want to hurry, and you got right back into your thick Iraqi accent." Nahlid put his arm around his friend's shoulder. "Take your time. Do things right. Your military training is progressing very well. You must learn the intricacies of establishing trust."

Shahidi looked at the ground, "I find it difficult to learn the infidel history of the United States because I do not understand it."

"Omar, you must look at their past as being the same as their present. They lack the one true God. You must see capitalism from the point of view of their Christian roots." He picked up an American history book. "Start at the American Revolutionary War. More wars follow. You will see that each war benefits those who wish to be rich making and selling articles used, related to, or in defense of war."

Shahidi turned a few pages, "I see that the first war of Independence involved a tax on whiskey and tea."

"Yes, you see, materialism is the foundation of Capitalism." Nahlid opened his tunic. "The infidel can only be persuaded by this." He pulled out a Beretta 9 mm pistol. "You do well with rifle and handgun. Your next training is with explosives. For this you will have to go to a special place."

"But what of my rice business. Who will keep it running and keep my workers honest?"

"Omar, we will take care of this as promised. We will supply you with money, food, and shelter while you are away. We will keep your business flourishing in your name. When anyone looks for Omar Shahidi, they will be told you are here busy with your work."

"We must talk of what will happen to my business if I go to Paradise." Shahidi rubbed his stubble chin.

"The necessary papers are ready for you to appoint relatives to help manage your affairs. They will be ready for your approval before you depart for Libya."

Chapter 10
The Stage Director

"Class I would like you all to meet Lorraine Domena. She's a stage director with a portfolio of over fifty dramas to her credit here in New York City." Cornish Bangdot stood aside for Domena to take the podium.

She was a six-foot well-proportioned female with yellow blonde hair pulled into a tight French twist. "Ladies and gentlemen, until now your behavior on the stage has been governed by the script and the script director. For films, the director relies on assistants who have various titles such as associate director or set director. My expertise is that of live theatre on a stage platform. The fine art of scenery, music, sound effects, entrances, and exits by the actors is very often the means to success of a play. Indeed, with the correct prompts, an actor's or actress's performance can be enhanced. Within the details of stage director is the all-important factor of timing. Timing in the theatre is as important as timing in life."

Winnie listened and processed each word. *The timing and the setting of events are indeed important.* She thought of her current situation with Father Nesbitt. She visualized Central Park.

A mugger would never have accosted them in front of crowds of people. Many would become, at the least, eye witness to the event and probably, also at the least, try to physically intervene. I wish I could tell this class about it. Our gunman, Malcom Flenk, used isolation to add fear and intimidation to his hold-up. Flenk had to turn us into victims. Winnie smiled at her next feeling. *I was afraid. Father Nesbitt was not. Father Nesbitt used confrontation and assertion to avoid being a victim.* She sighed, *Father Nesbitt is a true hero. How can any lawyer make the police or a jury think otherwise?*

Winnie heard her name being called by Domena. "Winifred Dorfinkle...what are your thoughts on my question?"

Winnie looked back at the stage director. "Could you please repeat the question?"

"Of course..." Domena waited a few seconds for a few chuckles to stop. "I mentioned how important scenery is to both the actor and the audience. Can anyone think of a situation where a play minimizes stage props to better a performance? What are your thoughts Ms. Dorfinkle?"

I hope my face isn't red. Her mind worked quickly, "Yes, I can visualize examples. First, Shakespeare used monologue soliloquy to concentrate on a single person—like in Romeo and Juliet. And even today, darkening a scene with a spotlight on a single performer...a singer...or an orator...for example."

"Absolutely correct Ms. Dorfinkle. I might add, and proceed to discuss, the use of costumes as actually setting up a mood and profile for a stage performer. For this, I like all to visualize Errol Flynn's Robin Hood. Your mind picture should be Robin dressed in forrest green with obvious large stitching suggestive of life in the rough. Now change the outfit to a cowboy suit."

The class laughed.

"Exactly, it doesn't work 100%." Domena continued with costume effects.

Winnie again flashed Malcom Flenk in her mind. He was a scruffy young man holding a gun, threatening murder. She changed the image to Father Nesbitt holding a gun and posing as a mugger. *It just doesn't work! How then can Flenk concoct a story that both she and Nesbitt were the criminals that day?*

ϟ

A small clutch of students surrounded Stage Director Lorraine Domena at the end of her two-hour teaching session. Winnie waited until she was alone with her.

"Ah…Ms. Domena, I have something really important to ask you." Winnie looked around and found the classroom totally empty.

Domena smiled, "You're Ms. Dorfinkle, right?"

"Wow, you remembered my name."

"Who can forget, 'Dorfinkle'"?

"It's Winnie…hmm…maybe I shouldn't get a stage name." She blurted. *There I go again coming out with something I hadn't intended to.*

"Well, Winnie, a name like Dorfinkle makes people smile. It's a funny name. In the theatre you don't want a funny name unless you're a comedian or want the stereotype of doing comedy the rest of your life." Domena gathered her notes and papers for her briefcase. "Is that what you wanted to talk to me about?"

"Oh...no...no... it might be much more important than that. I want to ask you if you have ever appeared in court as an expert witness about theatrical stuff?"

"I actually have, Winnie. Most of my legal attestations were related to accidents caused by faulty stage sets or failed props. One of my court sessions involved a play in which a dagger with a retractable blade failed to retract. It actually stabbed the star of the show. And when I phrase it like that, it appears that the dagger and not the person with the dagger is the culprit. The detectives then have to track who was responsible for the prop...the dagger. Is that what you mean?"

"Almost...sort of...well...no. I was thinking more of testifying that a victim didn't look like a crook and that a criminal looked and acted like what he was."

Domena's face paled. "I actually did. A defense lawyer kept relating to his client by repeatedly saying to the jury: 'Does this man look like a criminal...of course not.' In fact, the man looked scarier than Halloween."

"Did your expert testimony influence the outcome?"

"Yes, according to the District Attorney." Domena clasped her hands together. "Winnie, why are you asking me this?"

"Well, I'm personally involved in a mugging. I was the muggee along with a Priest. I'm scared that the man who threatened to kill us with a gun in Central Park can make good his story that we were the crooks and him the victim."

"Oh my God! Is this about the recent Central Park hold-up?"

"Yes, but I'm not supposed to talk about it. The gunman is claiming that Father Nesbitt and I were the robbers. He's actually suing me, the Priest, the Police, and the Catholic Church."

Domena sat down. "Winnie I was actually a victim like you. The mugger almost got off scot-free. It was only when I described what a criminal should look like on stage that we won the case and he went to jail. I'll never forget the look of hatred that man, Malcom Flenk, was his name, gave me."

Winnie's jaw dropped open and emitted only stuttering unintelligible sounds.

Nahlid looked out of the plane's dirty window and at the combat training camp they were flying over. *Omar Shahidi is probably looking up at my plane now. It is not pleasant down there. The reports have been good from his training.* Nahlid's vision became diminished as the plane's engines stirred up a small sandstorm to the side areas of the packed sand runway.

Two khaki-clad soldiers each shouldering an AK47, escorted Nahlid to an aluminum one story tan building. It had an arched quonset-hut roof attached to straight walls.

The front and back of the structure had a single door six-feet from a retractable garage-like entry to house large vehicles. Nahlid looked around at the enclosed four offices and at the two Russian tanks, two artillery pieces, and a wall lined with pallets of ammunition for small and large weapons. He pulled down the scarf covering his nose and lower face and smiled as Shahidi walked toward the air-conditioned office.

They exchanged greetings acknowledging Allah. Nahlid embraced Shahidi. "Omar, your arms and shoulders are hard and large now."

Shahidi felt self-confident, "I am comfortable with the weapons. I have passed all competence testing with them." He inhaled a deep breath as the door was closed to the cooler office space. He sat on a cushioned tan bench facing Nahlid.

"I think you know what my next words are to be." Nahlid folded his arms. Some fine sand puffed from his black fatigues and settled slowly to the dirt floor. Bottles of cold water were distributed to all four of the group.

Shahidi tightened his lips, "I am eager to go to a next action, which will bring me closer to the Navy Nesbitt."

Nahlid scanned some papers from Shahidi's evaluation file. "I am happy that your English has but a trace of accent. Your months here have made you effective with hand-to-hand confrontation as well as with small arms." He looked up from the report, "I see they now include training with poisons and knives."

Shahidi stiffened in his sitting position, "It was not difficult for me. With each piece of training I pictured Nesbitt as the receiver of my efforts. My faith has replaced fear."

"Omar, you are now indeed a soldier of Allah. You must now become a teacher of English to those of Islam who need such a skill."

With a puzzled look Shahidi looked at the others. "Teacher of language? Do you mean interpreter?"

"You will proceed to an area outside of London. The UK, like many other western countries is a site of relocation for a large number of Muslims. Most do not adhere to the directives of Al Qaeda or Bin Laden." Nahlid sat back and wiped his upper lip after a large gulp from his water bottle. "They are those who need to learn English, Spanish, French or other languages for successful blending with their new country's population. Your job will be teaching English. You will then receive credentials sufficient to enter the United States as a teacher of both English and Farsi. It is this identity that will get you close to the Navy Nesbitt."

Chapter 11
Malcom Flenk

Flenk had tried to reflect on his past and how to get his new lawyer on his side. He had two hours before the jailer came to escort him to the interview room. *What should I tell him? Should I begin in my childhood or focus on my felony-free record the past three years? Surely everyone has access to my criminal past.* He pulled down his folded sleeves. *Is it getting colder or am I sweating because I think any court-appointed lawyer won't be worth a shit—me with my record.* The bright orange shirt and pants identified him as a recent detainee and prisoner awaiting trial.

Thoughts began their parade, starting with his first felony. *God I was only six. I was in a Woolworth's store and stole a dozen small toys. No one was looking. I got nabbed at the exit door with the toys stuffed in my book bag. I would have gotten a dismissal of charges if I hadn't bitten the guy. I shouldn't have thrown a rock through the store window when I ran away. It was my parents' fault. Mom and dad both worked, but they never gave me anything. Especially dad, he was the worst.* Flenk thought back. He could hear his father with every one of his police confrontations.

"Mal, why can't you stop stealing? You're sixteen now and I can't do anything about you going to adolescent jail. You can get a job. You don't need to steal anything."

And his mother's words, "Why is God punishing me with such a criminal child? You won't go to church. You skip school. You get in fights. You use profanity like a second language. Is it my fault?" She would collapse onto a sofa sobbing on a pillow.

His dad would then lapse into his usual monologue, "Look what you're doing to your mother. You're a rotten child. You have no regard for the consequences of your actions."

His files with the police continued to accumulate, along with three short-term jail sentences. The last one was decreased, but it could've been enforced for the whole ten years. The conviction was the fault of that dipshit Broadway stage director. *What was her name...enema something? No, it was Domena.* He had a good lawyer for the appeal. The charge of aggravated robbery was an automatic ten years. Aggravated meant he used something that could be construed as a weapon. Armed robbery with a gun was the worst...twenty years in stir for a repeat offender. But his lawyer was successful. He convinced the Judge that robbery with a plastic fork did not constitute a life threatening felony, especially when no threat to the victim was made.

Flenk thought about that and applied it to his current situation with the Priest and the acting student. *All I said was "gimme your money"—the one with Domena. This time I did say I'll shoot you. I don't think I said I'll kill you. Yeah, I'll talk with the new lawyer and tell about the Domena lady. If I'm lucky and can convince the lawyer that my multiple lawsuits will net him great publicity, maybe he'll go for it.*

Flenk was escorted to the Lawyer-Client Interview room in handcuffs and leg-chains. His attorney, Rodney Ducette, was waiting at the solitary table surrounded by four chairs.

Ducette, in a vested, pin-striped dark brown suit, waited for Flenk to be seated. "Mr. Flenk, I'm your court-appointed attorney since you lack the resources to afford private counsel. Once I hear your story, I may ask for removal of your cuffs and shackles."

"I'm a reformed and law-abiding citizen, Mr. Ducette. I made some mistakes in the past, but can you believe anyone holding up a fake Priest and his whore?"

Ducette made a time-out sign with hands. "Hold it right there, son. First off, Father Nesbitt is a Priest in good-standing. Second, the girl was one of his Parish constituents. So, you can drop that confabulation right now. Just tell me what you were doing walking in Central Park on the day of your arrest."

"Jesus Christ Mr. Ducette, I was just out for a walk. It was a nice afternoon and I wanted to take a walk. But it seems you can't even do that anymore with a Priest and a woman who are muggers."

"Mr. Flenk, when you are asked to speak just state facts. Do not, I repeat, do not offer any opinion or editorials unless asked. Remember, it's the Priest and the young student who are accusing you. I need to know all about you."

Flenk sat back with a one word thought, *Fuck.*

⤙

Nahlid looked at his map of the United States. Small pins with red BB-size tops marked where his embedded immigrants were located. The green-topped pins where those who were tracking LCDR Nesbitt. The last report was from Florida. Nesbitt had been discharged from the Navy Hospital, but was reported as still in uniform.

Nahlid's cell phone vibrated. "Yes, what do you report?"

"The man Nesbitt went to a Veterans Administration Hospital for transition to civilian life." The transmission was choppy.

"Where in the United States is this hospital? How long will he be there? Is he still in the Navy?"

"The hospital is in State of New York. That is all we know right now. We have a tracker on him within the Veterans system and should know soon were he went from there."

Nahlid hung up. *It must be soon. Shahidi finishes his language-teaching training in a short time.*

Chapter 12
Father Nesbitt

Nesbitt's cell phone vibrated as he walked from the confessional. One thing he did like about confession was his need for total concentration on the confessor. The process took him away from preoccupation with his own troubles. Nesbitt answered his phone. The caller ID rectangle indicated "unknown caller".

"Father Nesbitt speaking."

"Is this also LCDR Forbish Nesbitt?" The voice was deep and direct.

"This is Father Nesbitt. Who may I ask is speaking?"

"This is Captain Delmore Craig. I'm calling from the Navy Central Security office."

Nesbitt took a breath as he continued to walk to his room behind St. Pats. He knew this Navy division. *Central Security deals with maintenance of secret Navy personnel data.* "I know the name Captain Craig. How do I know you're who you say you are?"

"Very good, Father Nesbitt, I want you to call me back by starting with the Navy Bureau of Separation Records. Find the numbers for yourself. If my call is for real, you will finally get to my office. Please be informed that what I have to say to you is extremely important. I'll hang up now with one more statement—your life depends on your returning my call as soon as possible."

&

Nesbitt went to his cell-like room. He unlocked his Navy duffle bag and took out his personnel file. He dialed the number for Navy Separation Records and identified himself.

"Captain Delmore Craig is not in this department Commander Nesbitt." It was a friendly female voice. "Hold on, I'll transfer you to Navy Discharge Operations."

"Your files are classified with Navy SEAL Special Operations personnel, sir. The best I can do is put you through to Navy SEAL Middle East Teams for the year you retired."

"Navy SEAL Team Bureau of separation records, how can I help you, sir."

Nesbitt frowned, "Captain Delmore Craig is expecting my call. This is former LCDR Forbish Nesbitt."

The phone rang twice and was answered with a deep bass voice, "Father Nesbitt this is Captain Delmore Craig."

"All right Captain, you have my attention." Nesbitt felt his pulse go up.

"I wanted you to go through the exercise of returning my call for you to take what I have to say seriously. First of all, anyone trying to reach me would have to know my name and where to find me. If the caller lacked appropriate military identifiers he or she would never have gotten past the first phone query. You were able to wade through this maze because you answered all such cues correctly."

Nesbitt's pulse slowed a little. "You can, of course, get an idea of alien queries to former service member files. Have you had any?"

"That's the gist of my call, Father Nesbitt. As of yesterday, a total of twenty-eight attempts have been made probing your current whereabouts. We've traced the callers. They never got past Navy Discharge Operations. A few phones were traced to landlines of known radical Islamic cells. Most were from within the US. Three were from Iraq, one from Libya, and four from a hamlet outside London."

"Well, what are they trying to find out, sir?" Nesbitt's pulse increased again.

"They want to know how to find you, Father Nesbitt. Recall that when you left the SEALs your discharge papers, including your addresses and current employment status, were declared top secret."

"It doesn't sound friendly, Captain. Do you have any feelings about this?"

"Father Nesbitt, your record of action with the Navy SEALs is outstanding. Your last action did result in casualties, including you. Knowing the Al Qaeda like I do, and I'm sure you do, you've been marked a target by jihadists related to that last mission."

"What should I do about it, sir?"

"For one thing, be on guard. To our best information, no one knows that Father Nesbitt is also the SEAL

Team leader of that action. What we'd like to do is find out the who and where all these callers are from and take them out of circulation."

"How can you accomplish that, Captain?" Nesbitt touched his crucifix, but he knew the answer.

"You can let us let them get through so we can track them."

"What if I say no?"

"Father Nesbitt, these people will eventually find you and hit you when you least expect it. If we can trace them, we might be able to get to them before they get to you or anyone close to you or your parish."

I knew it. Nesbitt inhaled deeply and said, "Captain, it's not only me I'm concerned about. I have constituents as a Priest. They would be in harm's way."

"They already are. If we can't protect you and those around you, the consequences could be devastating." Craig waited a few seconds. "Father Nesbitt, do you still have your SEAL duffle."

"Yes, sir."

"And your Beretta 9 mm?"

"Yes, sir."

"My office will send you a Federal permit to carry the gun. Are you okay with this?"

"How soon will I get the permit, Captain?"

"In three hours, I'll keep in touch, and Father. You're doing the right thing." He disconnected.

Across the crested waves of the Mediterranean, Nahlid pointed to a dusty pickup truck waiting outside the encampment. "First, I'm here to accompany you back to Iraq."

"It's been three months. It's hotter here in Libya than it is back home." Shahidi swallowed the last of his bottled water.

Nahlid smiled, "Good, you're speaking English. You must always speak English unless there is a purpose to speak Farsi. When you say back home where exactly are you from."

Shahidi smiled back, "Why in Duffield, England, just outside of London. Are we really going to Iraq before the UK?"

"Yes, you have papers that have to be notarized in Iraq. You have to be satisfied with your business and estate being left in trusting hands."

"Left? Will this be my last trip back home? Am I close to being ready to meet LCDR Nesbitt?"

They continued to sweat in the non-air conditioned pickup as the airport access roads appeared. "Omar, your speech is outstanding."

Shahidi laughed and coughed, "So much dust and loose sand here. My speech is better, yes. For the last three months they make us speak only English."

"Very good, I will tell you when to speak English after we arrive back in Iraq. Your first assignment will be in the Duffield, London suburb. It will be part of your training to move freely among English-speaking people. You will be learning how to behave and act like a language teacher as well as teach such classes."

"And after that?"

"I will tell you when the time is right."

"Will you tell me when you have located LCDR Nesbitt?"

"Yes…yes, I will tell you as soon as I know something that is correct. I must have all of your contact information once you leave for England." Nahlid paused then put his hand on Shahidi's shoulder. "And if you make additional contacts or get news from others you must inform me immediately."

Chapter 13
The Glycemic Index

Winnie was excited and couldn't wait to tell Father Nesbitt about Lorraine Domena. *Should I call him now? It's late afternoon and in two hours I'll be at my meeting with Dr. Potts and the next teaching session.* Winnie looked at the button on her cell phone ready to launch her call to Father Nesbitt. She spoke to the phone, "If I don't call you now, I won't be able to focus on the lecture." She initiated the call and waited for Nesbitt's pick-up.

Nesbitt felt the vibrating call alert on his belt-held cell phone. He looked at the caller ID. If it said unknown or a name he didn't know, he'd let them leave a message. He was relieved that it was Winnie. He was more than relieved. *Why do I look forward to any form of her presence?*

"Hello, Winnie. What's up?"

"Oh, Father Nesbitt, I think I have good news." Winnie's enthusiasm allowed Nesbitt to transfer his thoughts from Captain Craig's recent input. "Great, I can definitely use some positive thoughts right now."

"I just came from my theatrical class. It was all about stage acting, not movie or camera recorded situations. The professor was Lorraine Domena. Do you know the name?"

"The theatre is not my domain, Winnie. So what's the news?"

"Well, you know…actually you don't know because I haven't told you yet."

Nesbitt smiled, "Are you going to tell me. The suspense is killing me."

"Well, Domena is, and has been, an expert in jury trials involving criminals projecting as being threats. She says it's all measured by their appearance. I mean like in a mild, moderate to severe image classification. She's actually contributed to determining the degree of threat imposed by thugs of the mugger, and worse-types just by what they look like."

"What's so important about that?"

"One of the felons Domena helped convict via her testimony was Malcom Flenk." Winnie held her breath waiting for Nesbitt's response.

"Well, that is good news. Did you tell her of our situation?"

"Oh, she was well versed with the news media versions of our being mugged and that it was Malcom Flenk back in the saddle again. She didn't know that me and you are the key victims."

Nesbitt touched his crucifix, "God comes to our aid in strange ways, Winnie. Did you ask her if she might talk to our lawyers and the police of the possible use of her expertise—especially regarding Flenk?"

"I didn't have to, Father?" Winnie became silent.

"Well, Winnie what does that mean?"

"It means Father, that she volunteered to help in any way. She also said we should not behave like we are the criminals here. Flenk is on trial, not us. Her role would be to show us as victims and bring out the sociopathic felon nature in Malcolm Flenk."

"Winnie, you and I have to get together on this situation. Right now it's very important that we stay out of the media for a while. I can't explain it over the phone, but our lives would be in danger if a certain segment of the population knew where you and I lived."

"Father Nesbitt! Whatever do you mean? Our lives? I mean we've already been threatened by Flenk. He was going to kill us in Central Park." Winnie's voice became louder and higher pitched.

"Believe me Winnie, if we have to use your professor we will. But let's hold back right now. I'll explain later. And, what you've told me is good news." Nesbitt looked at his Navy SEAL issue Omega watch. "Can we meet at a crowded hamburger joint later this evening? You can pick the place."

Wow, that's almost like a real date. She took a deep breath. "There's a Fuddrucker's that's two blocks from my place and from yours. How about 7:30?"

"I'll see you there. Wear a jacket or sweater, it's supposed to be chilly this evening."

"Oh, yes, Father." *He's so wonderful, he even thinks of my welfare on a cold night.* "Oh, and Father, I have a class with Dr. Potts from five to six. I should be there on time."

Dr. Potts stood to the side of the tan wooden-frame podium. His long white lab coat, dark-rimmed glasses, and unruly thinning-brown hair still brought to mind a Woody Alan caricature. Winnie sat in front. She smiled at Potts as his unbuttoned white linen coat revealed a bright purple shirt and a yellow tie with white polka dots. He gulped a long swig from a Fiji water bottle.

"Today is one of the most important of our sessions." Potts burped and resumed as he wiped his mouth with his coat sleeve. "I'm talking about the Glycemic Index of foods. I trust you all have read the assigned pages in the hand-out packet you received on your first visit. You may refer to them as our discussion develops."

Potts allowed a half minute for the class to take out their glycemic readings. "Okay, so first, what is a Glycemic Index. In all simplicity, my dears, the Glycemic Index is a relative ranking of carbohydrate content in foods that once ingested and metabolized, will elevate your glucose (or sugar) levels. Now let's look at numbers. Having an index or list of foods with an index of 55 or lower are those whose carbohydrates are broken down slowly over time and are therefore absorbed slowly. Glucose triggers release of insulin which has two important pathways for your body to process the glucose in the blood. If glucose is slowly absorbed because of slow release it will most likely be used up for whatever activity you are doing while awake. If a large wad of glucose is released, the insulin summoned forth will direct the glucose to be stored for reserve energy as fat. Fat is our enemy. If you have a large meal and then go to sleep for the night, you will produce fat. I said fat. Think fat. Fat, Fat, Fat. Think about not making your biggest meal the one before bedtime. Do what the British do. Breakfast is the biggest meal with a snack for lunch and maybe a token of slow carbs at night."

Potts folded his arms as the eighteen class members stared at him open-mouthed, including Winnie. Seven of the attendees were men. He continued, "Part of the success of your training here is dietary awareness and knowledge. So let's look at some food stuffs and their glycemic index."

"Since most of you are theatre oriented, you undoubtedly partake of popcorn. Let's look at popcorn's glycemic index—72 for 2 cups of unbuttered popcorn. Add butter which is fat with extra calories, and the index increases to102."

Several "Oh, no" and separate expletives of "damn, shit, fuck, and balls" tainted the airwaves.

Potts loved this. It meant they were listening and their memory banks would store this vital way of thinking. He raised his palms for silence and spoke, "Let's go down the index table and look at potato chips with an index of 54 for 4ounces or a handful. And let's compare these chips to spaghetti at 42. Both foods are considered as starch products. Here, however, lies an important difference. Potato starch is rapidly metabolized to glucose and any unused glucose turned to fat. Pasta, however, is slowly broken down and most of the glucose burned up for energy un-less…" Potts tugged on his yellow polka dot tie. "…unless you stuff your pasta into your face just before you go to bed. Then most of your pasta digested carbs is stored as fat. Yes, I'll say it over and over again. Fat! Fat! Fat!" He walked around the podium waving his arms with each "Fat" expletive. "It's turned into extra you in the form of fatter upper arms, fat balloon like bosoms (for you girls), enormous cushy derrières, and not-so-lovely love handles for everyone. Picture yourself sitting on a toilet seat with twenty-five pounds of saggy, droopy, fleshy love-handle fat hanging down on either side of the limits of the toilet seat."

Winnie pictured herself as a fat circus freak munch-ing potato chips and shoveling spaghetti into her face smeared with tomato sauce. "Oh no." she shrieked.

Potts looked down from the podium. "Maintenance of your body shape and size is up to you. You are all here to gain control of your body."

Winnie looked at the wall clock. It was almost 6-o'clock. She had to meet with Father Nesbitt. All she could think of was, *What is the glycemic index of a hamburger?* Only the bun was carbohydrate. She raised her hand.

"Yes, Winnie."

"How do we compute the risks with a hamburger using the glycemic index?"

Potts beamed, someone always helped him with a question like that. It segued into future lectures. "I'm glad you asked. Remember the glycemic index is only for glucose...sugar...containing foods. For a hamburger only the roll is carbohydrate and with an index of 61. The rest of the burger is protein and fat. In those substances we speak of calories. However, that is a topic for future sessions." Potts looked down again at Winnie, "A glycemic index of 61 is over the desired 55. Adding protein calories is obtained by multiplying the grams of meat by 4 and for grams of fat by 9. Assuming a burger is bought at a fast food place the risk is the high glycemic index of bread or the roll with an average of 230 calories for meat and 180 calories for fat. If you eat it before bedtime you produce Fat! Fat! Fat!"

Omar Shahidi looked at his mirrored body after stepping from the shower. *The physical training of a soldier has made me turn my soft parts to hard muscle.* He flexed his arms. *I must continue to keep my body strong.* He almost jumped in place when the phone rang in his hotel room.

Shahidi picked up the phone and cradled it with both palms. *I pray to Allah that it is Nahlid with news about America and Nesbitt.* He spoke a soft "Hello" into the receiver.

"Ah, Omar, it is me, Nahlid. I am calling for several reasons. First, I had to test how you answer the phone. Your are in London now and in your acting as an English speaking bilingual Islamic you must not start a phone talk with words of our beloved Allah. You have passed the first test."

"It is good to hear your voice. You have news for me, Nahlid?" Shahidi tightened his hold on the telephone. The loud shrill shriek of the phone's ring still had him in a startle mode.

"Your words are in good English-speaking. That is my other reason for the call. Are you wearing the clothes sent in the case to your room?"

"Yes, the note in the suitcase told me not to wear my clothes from home."

"Exactly, Omar, you must dress like an English-speaking man. It adds to your credibility of being both an interpreter and a teacher of English."

"What are these black tight-fitting underthings for? For what purpose do I wear them?" Shahidi fingered a dark blue exercise muscle shirt and stretchable knee-length black shorts.

"They are not underclothes, my friend. Westerners engage in exercise via lifting weights, running on tread-mills, and using machines to maintain their muscle strength and size. Those are your fitness clothes. You will find a fitness center in all hotels we have for you. They are also to be used at such places of exercise in America, which are separate from the apartments where you will be living."

Shahidi thumbed through a folder containing sever-al files of papers and notes for teaching a transition from speaking Farsi to English. "I have my different pages to instruct non-English speaking Islamics and I have already given my first language class here in the London hotel. I found it very simple and pleasant to do this. I have never met such men with eagerness to learn the English speech."

Nahlid laughed, "You will find such students everywhere in your journey, especially in America. All of your classes contain many former soldiers who will continue their fight for Allah in the Western world. They wish to eliminate the infidels like those who killed your family and killed Islamic soldiers—people like Forbish Nesbitt. They are motivated by the one true God, Allah of the Koran. Some will even become martyrs for the honor and reward of paradise should they perish in such effort."

Shahidi looked back in the mirror still holding the phone to his left ear, "Yes, I know of this feeling." He took a deep breath. "Do you have news of where Nesbitt is?"

"Do not be in a hurry. You must develop a sense of comfort with being with the British and soon with the Americans. You manner, your dress, your food, your way with words must become natural to the people around you. You must work at eliminating your accent, although I must say your English-speaking is almost without accent as we talk today."

"Nahlid, my mentor here and those I have met since my training in Libya insist on all of us speaking English and using our native dialects only for Salat."

"It is to be like this until you return to your home, Omar. You may speak Farsi or Iraqi only during your prayers." He paused. "At this time, I can tell you that Al Qaeda has placed our people in two places where Nesbitt has been since his injuries at your home. These chosen ones will point us in the direction of where he is now."

"But Nahlid, surely once you locate him, I must quickly destroy this man."

"No, it must not be like that. His last known Navy placement was in Orlando, Florida. His wounds from what happened in your house received their final treatment. We don't know the details of where he went from there. Omar, you are not to worry, we will arrange your confrontation to have the most exposure possible. The world must know that Nesbitt killed your mother and father. Our world must learn that your brother, a true soldier of Allah, was avenged."

Chapter 14
Hamburger Heaven

Winnie lingered after Dr. Potts' class. She was the last of three who had a question for which they wanted only private interaction with mentor Potts.

"Yes, Winnie my dear, what is on your mind?" Potts raised his eyebrows, wrinkling his brow and at the same time wiggling his right ear. The motions tilted his dark-frame glasses making him look as idiotic as Woody Allen in his most comedic movie.

"Dr. Potts, I'm about to do something I know I shouldn't. I feel so guilty after today's lecture on glycemic foods." She started to wring the sleeves of her pink woolen jacket as she stared at him. She was caught between feeling the nervousness of confession and urge to laugh at his ridiculous clothes and expression.

"You just learned of the Glycemic Index this past hour. What could you possibly feel guilty about?"

"I don't know, I mean, talking to you like this I feel like I'm talking to a priest during confession." She looked at the floor. "And Dr. Wood...Dr. Potts...it's not really about glycemic foods. Well, I mean it is but it's more than that. I have a date tonight at a restaurant which serves food that my body would only turn into fat."

Potts started to laugh. "A date? With whom, where, and which restaurant?"

"Well, I have a date with a Catholic Priest." She lifted her gaze from the floor to look at his cow eyes and crooked glasses. "We're going to eat at Fuddruckers—cheeseburgers and french fries."

Potts couldn't control his laughter. He held on to his slight paunch-belly, which shook with small Santa Claus-like rippling waves. "A date with a priest? Fuddruckers?" Tears were starting to form as his laughter continued.

Winnie put her hands on her hips letting her pink jacket fall to the floor. "I don't see any humor in my situation. I mean, look at the french fries, they're almost pure starch and fried. And what about the burger with its grease, cheese and roll? What am I to do?"

Potts stopped laughing. "I can't advise anything about the Priest. I mean that, my dear, is about the safest date a girl can have. As for the meal, well, let me just say, and I am very sincere in what I'm about to impart, the solution is very easy."

"Easy?" Her thoughts turned to Woody Allen. *I wonder what Woody Allen is really like.*

"Living in New York most of my adult life, I have gotten to know every type of restaurant and what kind of alternative food-rescues exist. By the time you finish your first year with my teachings, you will lose all worry and fear about eating." Potts scratched his left armpit.

"First, you are not to order a burger or fries. Second, you will order an alternative meal. I, my dear, dear, dear Winnie…" Potts put his right arm around her shoulders. "…am familiar with Fuddrucker's menu items. You may order a low calorie salad and iced or hot Green Tea. The salad will provide appropriate nourishment and the Green Tea will prevent any excess calories from turning into fat."

"But what if my date insists on my ordering the burger and fries."

"Dearest Winnie, he's a Priest." Potts stopped and rubbed his chin. "How old is this Priest?"

"About two years older than me. What has his being a Priest got to do with our eating?" Winnie pulled on her court jester knit hat.

"As a Priest, he's bound by his sacred vows to think pure thoughts. He will respect your opinions and honor whatever you want to order from the menu." Potts stepped back. "Winnie, why did you make a date with a Priest…and at Fuddruckers?"

"I didn't."

"What do you mean you didn't?"

"He asked me, Dr. Potts"

"Why?" Potts started to sweat under his nose.

"Why? Because he said if he didn't talk to me face-to-face tonight, we might be murdered."

"Winnie, maybe you should cancel the date with this Priest." Potts followed her to the door as she put on her pink jacket.

"I can't cancel the date. The whole purpose of our meeting is to find out how not to get murdered. Anyway, thanks for talking to me, Dr. Potts. I gotta go."

Potts shouted after her, "Don't forget, order the low-cal salad and the Green Tea."

Winnie found the two block walk to Fuddruckers in the blowing cold and forceful wind something that in her mind might qualify as a near-Alaska winter experience. And it was only October. She got there less than two minutes before Nesbitt.

"I almost didn't recognize you Father, You look like a terrorist with that navy blue watch cap, long winter coat, pink mittens, and that black scarf wrapped around your face."

Nesbitt slowly unwound the scarf and pulled off his mittens. He kept his coat and hat on.

Winnie stared at him. "You look like a homeless person." She smiled, "Where'd you get the pink mittens, Father?"

Nesbitt looked at her and laughed, "I couldn't find my gloves so I scrounged though the sanctuary's lost and found. These were the only things that fit." He reached over and snipped two fingers at one of her hat's jester bobbing things with a little bell on it. "You look like the court jester who almost froze to death."

"I got this hat at a flea market in Central Park during a snow storm two years ago. It's warm and makes me look underage. I wear it as a potential molester repellant. I shoulda wore it the day we got mugged."

"Winnie, let's get our food and sit down in the back where there's privacy."

There was no line and they looked at the menu postings on the wall behind the counter. Fuddrucker's smelled of overused frying fat mixed with pig's knuckles molten gelatin.

Nesbitt ordered his cheeseburger with everything on it, a double order of fries, and hot black coffee. Winnie looked at the menu and finally made her choice.

"I'll have the dieter's salad without croutons and a large hot Green Tea."

Nesbitt made no comment.

⤙

There were only a few occupied tables close to the counter. They kept their warm clothes on. It seemed cold at the rear of the restaurant. "There must be a crack in the wall, Father. It's breezy and cool back here."

"We can talk while we eat, Winnie. I hope I didn't scare you during our phone conversation. What you told me was really important and what I'm going to tell you is not only important, but it's also secret. You can't tell anyone what I'm about to tell you."

"As secret as the confessional stuff, huh Father?" the meat smell of his Fuddrucker's specialty almost made her drool.

"Even more so, Winnie." His first bite consumed a third of the burger. Nesbitt used two napkins to wipe the juice sliding off his mouth.

Winnie sat forward and spoke in a low tone, "So, how come people shouldn't know who we are? I mean what people?"

"Winnie, it's not so much you, as me."

"You, you're just a Priest at St. Patrick's in New York."

Nesbitt leaned across the table, "I wasn't aways a priest. Before you called, I was contacted by a former friend from when I was in the Navy."

"Were you a Priest in the Navy?"

"No, Winnie, I was serving with combat troops in Iraq. My unit went on many covert operations."

"Covert? What does that mean? I mean in the Navy weren't you a sailor on a ship?"

"No, I was part of the Navy that operates on land."

"You mean like the Marines?"

"No, Winnie, I was a Navy SEAL."

Winnie's mouth dropped open. "Wow, no wonder you had no trouble with Malcom Flenk."

"I'm afraid my past will all come out with this mugging case if it gets sensational coverage by the tabloids."

"Did you do something bad, Father ?"

"Not bad by wartime standards. I did my job. I did it well. Let me tell you about my phone call today. The Department of the Navy called to warn me not to be in the public eye. There are people from actions I led in Iraq and elsewhere who are looking for me."

"Why is that bad…oh, oh…there the ones who want you dead." Winnie gulped her not so hot Green Tea.

"Right now, I'm told certain queries have been made by hostile sources who want to find me. The inquiries are sourced as being known terrorist groups. Winnie, one thing people in the States don't hear about is that the enemy in Iraq and Afghanistan are vengeful extremists. The war over there is a religious war, The jihadists believe in more than an eye-for-an-eye. Some of us, marked as leaders, are singled out for revenge in the hope that such acts will get great publicity and instill fear—terror—over here against us who they refer to as infidels. They wait until their single target is found and located in a crowd. Then a bomb goes off and many are killed."

Winnie sat back, "So, if Lorraine Domena goes public, your identity is flashed over the media and anyone associated with you gets to be part of the exploded stew."

Nesbitt folded his arms, "You have truly grasped the scenario. Our best hope is to deflect all attention away from us and onto Flenk, but without our names or pictures getting any press."

"How are we gonna do that?"

"I don't know yet, Winnie. Do you have any other questions?"

She reached over to touch his right hand. "Yes, do you have a tattoo? Oops, I asked you this before. You avoided an answer."

"A tattoo?" He raised his eyebrows. "Yes, Winnie, as I told you I do have a tattoo from my Navy days."

"Can I see it?"

"Here?"

"Yes, unless it's someplace embarrassing."

"I can't get at it with all these clothes on."

"Oh, really?"

"Honestly, Winnie, do you understand that everything we talked about is not for publication. Our lives and the lives of people we don't even know depend on it."

"Even about the tattoo?"

Nesbitt stood up, wrapped his scarf around his neck and lower face and put his pink mittens on. "It's time to leave." He watched her walk ahead of him. *Why do I not want to see her go?*

Chapter 15
The Pedagogue

Shahidi was ambivalent with his feelings toward television. His village did not have television for other than political broadcasts. It was told that *Commercial TV demonstrates the social excesses of the western world.* He looked at the TV screen in his hotel room. It was a flat screen, not like the large picture-tube units usually available to the public back home. He held his finger over the mute button as he listened to the weather report. A well groomed man and woman were alternating the delivery of the news and weather. The woman announced, "London this October offers more cold, gray, rainy, and foggy days than any other Octobers of weather documentation." The forecast for today concluded with the same non-sunny expectation.

Shahidi pressed the mute to block out the commercials. He looked for an American station and selected one called *The Smithsonian Channel.* The program he wanted to watch was giving him an insight to what Americans were like, how and where they lived. It was called Aerial America. The State of Arizona was the episode's chosen selection.

The TV program voice was a baritone male, "Arizona boasts of having one of the wonders of the world in their borders. Yes, indeed, the Grand Canyon attracts over two million tourists each year."

Shahidi brought up a map of US states to his laptop. *What was it Nahlid had told me about Nesbitt? Yes, he was sent to a Navy hospital in Florida. If Florida is his home US place, he could still be there.*

Shahidi looked at his first language class tutorial. He wore tan slacks, brown loafers, and a white shirt with solid blue tie. His Irish greenish-blue Tweed sportcoat finished his continental appearance. Enrollment records showed his pupils were ages from 23 to 72. He went to the white board and wrote in bold letters: **From Farsi to English**.

Shahidi spoke in Farsi, "If this is not the course you signed up for please go to the administration office for correct placement."

No one left.

"Okay, I see that we have twenty students for this course. Since our classes will go for three months, you will do better if we get to know each other."

The class members looked around the room at their seated peers.

"We will speak only two languages, Farsi and English." He paused and pointed to a young woman in the first row to his left. "We'll start with you. State your name, where you are from, and why you want to learn English first using Farsi. Then say the same words in English. I'll write your Farsi introduction on the board. Then you try the English. This way we'll all benefit from each other's speaking."

The young lady in a drab gray full length dress stood, took a breath, and said in Farsi, "My name is Toriba. I am from Somalia. I must learn English to become American citizen and live near my family who are also such citizens."

Shahidi wrote her Farsi words on the Board. "Very well, Toriba, now you will, with the class's help, write the English word beneath each Farsi word."

The entire two hour class time was taken up by the twenty separate introductions. Shahidi was satisfied. Each student had learned how to speak English on their first day. He congratulated them. "Each day we have class, we will use more and more English and less and less Farsi. It will be just like today. Your assignment for the next class is to tell us what you like the most about London and what you like the least about London. You are also to read Chapters one through three in your language book and do the exercises at the end of each chapter. I will collect your written answers at the beginning of each class."

The woman called Toriba waited for the others to leave and went up to him. She spoke in Farsi, "I thank you for showing how I will learn the English-speaking."

"I think you will accomplish enough English vocabulary in three months to have an understanding and be able to speak with your American relatives."

She smiled and gave a little bow.

I too have a sense of accomplishment. Seeing my effectiveness as a language teacher is pleasing. I must pray to Allah for the patience to be ready for my sojourn to the United States by the end of this three month class.

Professor Cornish Bangdot finished his lecture on matching expressions with projected moods.

Winnie had done exceptionally well with anger, happiness, and tiredness. The anger part was easy. All she had to do was think of Malcom Flenk and she got mad. Being happy was another feeling she had no trouble with. A vision of Father Nesbitt and their proposed next meeting took care of that. Tiredness was something she actually felt. Her life right now was fraught with full time activities, which were physically and mentally exhausting.

Bangdot leaned on the small podium and asked, "Does anyone have any questions about human behavior as it might relate to an actor or actress?"

No one raised their hand except Winnie. "Yes, professor, why do people get tattoos and do their tattoos say something about who they are?"

Bangdot smiled, "Very interesting question, Winifred. Can you give me an example of what you're thinking about?"

She was excited and nervous at the same time, "Oh yes, I mean, say for example a Catholic Priest has a military tattoo. What might that person who represents peace and love really be like"

"My dear young lady, I love your example. It shows us that all people are capable of reinventing themselves. Your Priest might have a military past of blood and violence, which pushed him into a life of celibacy and the teachings of Jesus, the Prince of Peace. You will find in your acting roles you are in fact always reinventing yourself as someone else."

"Thank you professor, I'll be more discerning now when I evaluate people with tattoos." She sat down the remaining few minutes of the class. *I like Professor Bangdot's explanation—all except the celibacy part.*

Chapter 16
Detective Bauman NYPD

"Father, I must see you and Ms. Dorfinkle again at Police Plaza," Lt. Norman Bauman opened his appointment calendar.

Nesbitt was at his computer when his cellphone rang, "Let me call up my schedule, Lieutenant. Do I detect a sense of urgency?"

"Somewhat, it's more of a complication that has arisen, Father. I'd like to see you and the Dorfinkle woman apart and together on an agreed upon time."

"Okay, tomorrow is Thursday. I have from three o'clock on free." Nesbitt also looked at Friday. "Friday morning is also available."

"Good, I'll get back to you after I contact Ms. Dorfinkle." Bauman disconnected and punched in Dorfinkle from his speed dial list.

Winnie was leaving the college main entrance when her phone rang. "Winnie's phone. Winnie speaking."

"Detective Bauman, Winnie, I'm calling to arrange an appointment with both you and Father Nesbitt…separate and together. Father Nesbitt gave me his available times."

Winnie's pulse accelerated. *Father Nesbitt! Oh, I can't wait.* "Lieutenant, is four o'clock tomorrow, Thursday, okay? And where will we be meeting?"

"Yes, Winnie, that will be good. I need us to meet at my office at Police Plaza."

"The subway should get me there early. Is it something important?"

"Everything to do with your case is important, Winnie. Something has come up that both you and Father Nesbitt must be made aware of."

"Oh, it sounds scary. Am I in danger or something?" Winnie reflexly looked around outside the college entrance.

"It's nothing imminent. But it is something that will affect your safety."

Winnie responded in a high pitched voice, "Does it affect Father Nesbitt too?"

"Actually, it affects him more than you. I'll see you both tomorrow at four." Bauman hung up, He sat back in his squeaky chair with one thought. He spoke to his empty office, "The Navy, the Church, New York, terrorism, and one sleaze-bag mugger—what a situation."

Bauman looked at his notes. The Department of the Navy had called him late last evening at his home. It started after the first sip of what he hoped would be a soothing martini. His wife picked up on the first ring.

"Bauman residence. Belinda speaking." Belinda Bauman was a well kept fortyish woman who was totally used to her husband's life as a police officer. Lately, most of the phone calls after hours were for her. This one wasn't.

"I have to speak to Detective Lt. Norman Bauman please. It's extremely important. This is Captain Delmore Craig calling from the Department of the Navy."

Belinda handed her husband the phone. "It's the Navy. You better not enlist," She smiled as he took the call.

"Detective Lt. Bauman here."

"Lt. Bauman, this is Captain Delmore Craig. I was LCDR Nesbitt's commanding officer when he served with the Navy SEALs."

Bauman groaned and felt his bowels tighten. "I was going to call the Navy later on this week. Is this about his being mugged in Central Park?"

"Yes and no." Craig let out an audible sigh. "I'll give you the 'yes' part first. The Navy is concerned that the publicity about the New York incident will be problematic."

"Problematic for who? The Navy or Nesbitt…or me?"

"Lt., I'm afraid this is complicated. First, let me say that LCDR Nesbitt served honorably in the Navy. He was a top notch and decorated combatant. His spirituality was stimulated after his last action during which he almost got killed by a suicide bomber."

"Well, it is important that he's without any negative incidents on his record. The mugger in this case is claiming that Nesbitt initiated the Central Park assault."

"I know just a little about your case, Lt., however, Nesbitt would never be evolved in any criminal action. In fact, his training would only be triggered if he felt his life or someone else was in danger."

"Captain Craig, Nesbitt and a parish member were held at gunpoint during a robbery attempt. Nesbitt overpowered the criminal and sent him to the hospital."

"Do you have the weapon and any witnesses?" Craig asked.

"No witnesses, and yes we have the gun. The perp also has a long criminal sheet. My problem, and maybe yours, is that this is New York City. Lawyers are like sharks here. The perp has a lawyer who wants to make a name for himself. The press also loves this kind of situation. The lawyer is reversing the event sequence of events saying Father Nesbitt and the girl attacked him in an armed robbery attempt. The lawyer is bringing suit against the Catholic Church, Nesbitt, the young woman, and, although it hasn't happened yet, talks of blaming Nesbitt's Navy past for the entire situation."

After a few seconds silence, Craig responded, "I was afraid of something like this. Actually, our problem is that LCDR Nesbitt's last action, the one that almost took his life, placed his name on a jihad-fascist terrorism list. They're looking for him. They want him dead, and don't care about any collateral damage."

"Can they find his whereabouts from the Navy?"

"No, Lt., but they can from the church and from the press. I might add they could also try to reach into the NYPD for information. From our perspective, everything about LCDR Nesbitt's Navy career is classified except his honorable discharge."

"So I get everything else? Captain, I have limited resources at Police Plaza. Isn't there anything the Navy can do to protect him and the girl?"

"The Constitution forbids the military from such domestic actions. However, I'm putting together something for an Agency which can help. Bureaucracy delays may be as long as two weeks from today."

Bauman let out a moan, "Agency? Please don't say FBI. They hate New York City and the NYPD will lock horns with them."

"No, Lt. Bauman, this falls under the umbrella of the CIA. I'm working as fast as I can with this. You must also do everything you can to squelch this lawyer and the press."

"That's proving to be very difficult, Captain." Bauman wiped his sweating hands on his small martini napkin.

"Almost every military operation has impossible connotations, but we get the job done. If you can get that perpetrator convicted 'post-haste' as you police say, the better for Nesbitt, the girl, and all concerned. I'll keep in touch." Craig ended the call.

Bauman gave the phone back to his wife. He guzzled the remnants of his martini and uttered only two words, "Why me?"

Chapter 17
Police Plaza

Thursday afternoon couldn't come fast enough for Winnie. She had a chaotic time deciding on what to wear. With no speaking roles at school all she had to do was critique the readings of several of her classmates along with other selected members of the class.

I could wear pedal pushers and a fluffy turtle neck sweater. Or maybe I should wear something more conservative like for court. No, maybe a dress. She considered her options. *No not a dress, it'll make me look too young for Father Nesbitt. I'll just wear dress slacks, a colored blouse, and a button-down gray sweater.*

All during class her thoughts switched from Detective Bauman's warning about her and Father Nesbitt's safety to the acting students during their theatrical readings. The sessions ended by three o'clock and she rushed out of the building to the subway station.

She eyed the subway passengers with suspicion and fear. *Maybe the mugger has mugger friends who want her to admit that Father Nesbitt and me are the criminals. If I don't, maybe I'll be killed or worse. Yes, worse, I could have acid thrown in my face. My acting career will be ruined. Oh, dear God please don't let it be acid!*

Winnie arrived at Bauman's spartan, cluttered office at quarter-to-four. Father Nesbitt was already present and sitting across from Bauman. She was directed to enter and sit in a folding bridge chair next to Nesbitt.

⤚

Bauman sat back after shaking Winnie's hand. "I'm glad you both came early. As it turns out, I don't have to have separate audiences with each of you." He folded his hands and offered them both a bottle of chilled water. "We shouldn't be long. I want to be first let you both know that Mr. Flenk has signed a plea bargain against his lawyer's advice."

Nesbitt uncapped his water bottle, took a long swig, and leaned forward. "Plea bargain? Flenk has admitted to his actions?"

Winnie looked from Nesbitt to Bauman., "What kind of a plea bargain?"

Bauman opened a case file. "Mr. Flenk realizes that this offense, if he's found guilty, will make him a lifer in prison. It'll be his third conviction. His lawyer and the DA's office will lower the penalty to less than five years in prison with possible early parole if he drops all his frivolous suits and attests that your testimonies are accurate."

Nesbitt folded his arms, "How did this all happen?"

"Father, and Winnie, strange things occur in New York City. The Mayor's office received an overwhelming number of communications both from American church aficionados and from the Vatican. The Pope does not want to establish precedent with such lawsuits. The Church has suffered enough with the 'Gay Priest Phenomena' of recent times. In addition, the Mayor himself does not want New York City to allow creeps like Flenk to nurture lawyers' quests for money and fame. He feels, along with the Chamber of Commerce, that actions like this would affect tourism and change the image of our safe streets. The Governor also can't stand the tabloid press which thrives on smear campaigns." Bauman took a breath and a sip from his cup. "The clincher, however, was Judge Dewey Deuser. Deuser is up for reelection and wants good press. He'll favor the plea bargain, almost guarantee it."

Winnie breathed an audible sigh of relief, "Well, that's good news, isn't it?"

"Yes, that's the good news. The Governor's office has ordered the tabloids to retract their statements and publish the truth." Bauman hefted his large coffee cup and took three swallows. "Here's the bad news. I received a call from the Department of the Navy."

Nahlid waited for the sixth ring and hung up. He dialed again and hung up on two rings. The third call was picked up on a single ring.

"You are ready for your next journey." Nahlid paused to hear the expected reply.

"What is Allah's will?" Shahidi made a slight bow to the East.

"We have made a list of possible locations for the Navy SEAL. Our military, Veteran's Administration, and Washington DC agents, under the guidance of Allah, were able to track LCDR Nesbitt's movements within this United States."

Shahidi shuddered, "But that is not a favorable thing for me."

"Omar, you must look at the positive side of life as you go forward. Allah has intervened. The information I just told you is good. It told us that Nesbitt is no longer in the American Navy employ."

"I will bow to Allah's wisdom. Please tell me of my next assignment." Shahidi sat down and controlled his breathing. *I must trust and believe the all-knowing one.*

"Please let me continue. I will tell you that you are to go to New York City. You will meet a cell member who will explain your last item of training."

"America! I am going to America!" Shahidi stood up and could feel a droplet of sweat descend under his right armpit.

"Yes, our list included many more possible outcomes for the whereabouts of Nesbitt. I received earlier this week from one of our embedded agents in Vatican City that Nesbitt yes he is no longer a soldier. He is much worse. Your work is now elevated in importance. Nesbitt has become a Priest in the Catholic Church. He is the worst kind of infidel. He will preach that it is glorious to strike down those of Islam."

"How will I gain access to Nesbitt?"

"The details will be from your next director in New York."

Chapter 18
The Cell

Shahidi couldn't sleep on the British Airways flight from London to New York City. He was ticketed in First Class on a 747 jumbo plane and had complained to Nahlid. "The cost of this ticket is many times that of a Coach passenger. Mohammed preaches that Allah does not want us to squander money which could be best directed for other jihad purpose."

"We must consider your station, Omar. You are now a trained teacher and interpreter of our language. You are a person valued by infidels who need such a one as you have become. For you to travel in a lower privilege of seating might draw suspicion and endanger you and our jihad mission, which is of great importance for Islam."

Shahidi mellowed with his mentor's rationale. He looked at other first class passengers and cringed with anger. They seemed to have no difficulty settling in the reclining seats to sleep for the entire five hour flight. Just before takeoff, a stewardess approached him and the woman sitting next to him.

"Ma'am, would you like coffee, tea, fruit juice, water or champagne once we're airborne?"

"Champagne, of course. This is first class, after all." The dark-haired middle-aged woman sounded smug and aloof. She stared at Shahidi as the same choice was offered to him.

"I will have water, please." His words were deliberate and with barely a trace of foreign accent. *Westerners defy our teaching that a man must first be approached before a woman. And that woman and her privileged attitude. I hope Allah does not strike this plane down from the air with so many infidel decadents aboard.*

He accepted a blanket and assistance with converting his chair into a chaise lounge format for sleeping. However, sleep did not happen. A few who also did not sleep partook of a forbidden meal of meat, cheese and more wine. The flight attendant did put together an acceptable salad for him. *I hope this food choice does not make me suspect as a Muslim.*

One hour out of Kennedy International Airport, an attendant helped him fill out a foreign duty form. He felt sweat developing as they disembarked into the long line of travelers at the customs check-in.

The uniformed officer looked at Shahidi's passport picture and looked closely at him. The passport was examined quickly as there were few flights stamped on it. "What is the nature of your coming to the United States, Mr. Shahidi?"

Shahidi's mouth went dry. "I am a teacher of Farsi and English for Middle Eastern citizens." *I hope my words do not sound rehearsed.*

"I see your address is just outside New York City." The agent smiled. "Suffern, New York, I know this town. Its name does not indicate any 'suffering'. It has a very affluent and diverse population." He stamped Shahidi's passport and other documents. "You may proceed to collect your luggage through the next set of doors. Welcome to the United States."

Shahidi looked over his shoulder at the customs booth as he approached the baggage arrival area. *The Officer does not look back at me. He was friendly. I have succeeded so far.*

He walked slowly looking at the crowd of people at the roped-off reception area. Many held cardboard placards with names of people they were meeting. He scanned the men and woman who had anticipatory smiles as they looked at the passenger arrivals. One rectangular card with large dark red letters spelling his name caught his eye. The man holding the card looked serious. Shahidi waved to him and approached him trailing his one suitcase and smaller cary-on. The man's countenance immediately changed to a smile returning the wave.

The words of warning from Nahlid echoed in his memory. "If your greeter speaks to you in Farsi, do not connect with him. It will mean he his under surveillance."

The greeter looked at Shahidi. "Welcome, Omar Shahidi. Let me take one of your bags. We will walk together to the car. I am Ramik Zamir."

English, praise be to Allah. Shahidi smiled and shook the offered hand.

~

"Father Nesbitt, I had such terrible thoughts that Flenk had henchmen who would be after us. The NYPD plea bargain is such a relief." Winnie clutched Nesbitt's sleeve as they went together to the subway station.

Nesbitt fastened up his top black overcoat button and touched her hand at his sleeve. "There will still be a lot of publicity while the media retracts their words."

"But they won't mention us by name anymore, will they?" She moved closer to him after they passed through the turnstile to the subway car waiting platform.

"Of course they will, for the same reasons they got front page press before. The Church, the military, New York's Central Park, and now they can smear a little notoriety against lawyers. Flenk's lawyer is almost as sleazy as Flenk is." He grabbed her arm as she almost slipped on a wet spot on the uneven subway concrete.

"But it'll exonerate us as truly being victims, Father." She hung on to his hand.

"Yes, but if someone is looking for me and we're on the headlines, they're bound to find us. The jihadists have people embedded throughout the US. If Al Qaeda is searching for me, they'll have put the word out. We know that because the Navy has already detected a probe of Islamic extremists trying to find me." Nesbitt allowed the hand holding.

"Can you tell me about what happened over there? I mean, why would someone have such a grudge against a wartime event?" Her eyes fixed on his.

"Someday I'll tell you…maybe. It's still a classified SEAL operation." He moved back a few feet with her as the train's brakes made squawking noises covering further conversation. They moved into the car with the forward momentum of the five o'clock rush hour crowd.

Ramik Zamir did not offer spontaneous conversation. Shahidi looked at his new environment. Traffic was moving but it was slow until they got off the Tappen Zee Bridge. It was chilly outside and most pedestrians could see their breath. *I have been wise to heed Nahlid's advice of bringing a heavy coat and winter clothes.*

After 40-minutes Shahidi spoke, "Is this place, Suffern, what they call suburbs?" He looked at the stubbled Zamir who kept his eyes on the road.

"It is what some consider a bedroom community to New York City. There are both private homes and high rise apartments. There is a train connection, which has two express times that could get to the City in 45-minutes."

"Are there not cells of our people in the City itself?"

"Yes, and we would only use them after a New York City operation if travel outside of the City was closed off— like it was in the 9/11 attack." Zamir turned off the state highway and into the main street entering Suffern. "Our safe house is a private home in a predominantly Islamic neighborhood."

"Wouldn't that be dangerous for us if an action happened in the New York area?" Shahidi looked at the older wooden single story and two-floor private homes. "The houses are not of stone like mine."

"No, this part of the US has many Islamic communities. There is a Mosque near our house." Zamir flicked on the turn signal and slowed down.

"How many people will be in our house?" He suddenly felt vulnerable.

"Only four will be in your house. It is a two-family house. You have been profiled to blend in with such family units in this town. There will be you and I together and two others living in the attached second side."

Shahidi's pulse quickened. *Allah works in strange manners. Why do Americans accept us without suspicion or contempt?*

Chapter 19
Dr. Myron Potts

"Well, how'd it go, roomie?" Whitney Zotle waited until Winnie settled.

Winnie explained the new Flenk situation and the plea bargain details.

"So, the final outcome depends upon this Judge Doosey's decision?" Zotle opened a bag of potato chips and started munching.

Winnie reached into the bag and plucked a few chips. "Deuser not Doosey, yeah, the plea bargain obviates a jury trial. I guess seeing his future as life in prison verses something a lot less is a great deal. I mean, with his criminal thinking and all." She stuffed the chips into her mouth.

"Didn't you tell me that 'potato anything' is on your never eat glycemic index. What'll Dr. Potts think?"

Winnie grabbed a bottle of water from the fridge and took two swallows before answering. "Oh my God, you're right. And my next group meeting with Potts is tomorrow night." She stood before the floor length mirror and scanned her figure. "Well, this is my only recent food violation. It shouldn't impact on my movie-star body." Winnie flopped down on her bed with a frown.

"What's the matter now? You should be happy overall." Zotle looked in the same mirror and accepted her lumpy reflection with raised eyebrows and upward palms.

"Father Nesbitt told me I should also tell about the bad news we got from NYPD. I mean, I have to warn people close to me—like you." Winnie jumped up from the bed. "Oh my God, that includes Dr. Potts."

"Oh for God's sake what's the bad news?" Zotle put her hand into the chip bag.

Winnie whispered, "Father Nesbitt and I have become targets."

"Why are you whispering? There's only the two of us here, Winnie." Zotle's mouth turned down. "What kind of target?"

Winnie explained about Nesbitt's Navy Middle East combat and how the outcome of one of his battle actions turned bad. "An Iraqi survivor might be stalking him for assassination. And Whit, those kind of extremists don't care much about collateral damage. They might shoot or blow-up anyone close to Father Nesbitt just to kill the good Father."

Zotle swallowed several gulps of water. "We'll just have to try to distance ourselves from each other." She rubbed her chin. "But how do we do this in our apartment?"

"I was thinking of commuting from my home in Connecticut so I wouldn't be here for a terrorist who wants to get information from me about Father Nesbitt."

"All that would accomplish is to put your parents in jeopardy. No, we should just leave things as they are. If I'm interrogated I wouldn't know anything about Nesbitt."

Winnie was silent, thought, and then added, "No, that wouldn't work. If they were looking for me they'd torture you for my whereabouts."

Zotle sat next to her roommate on her bed. "So, Winnie, our best bet is to ask for protection by the NYPD. They could post a guard here or something."

"We asked about that. Detective Bauman doesn't have the available staff. But Father Nesbitt is thinking about asking the Navy for some protection."

Zotle smiled, "Yeah, I'd love to have a few sailor SEALs around."

"I'll keep you informed on what happens with that."

Dr. Myron Potts stood beside the podium with his long white coat open as usual. The class of a dozen patients, including Winnie were all smiles. Potts' hair was in Woody Alan style with the hair from his temples splayed out sideways like accessory wings. His dark rimmed glasses and clueless expression preceded his opening remarks, which completed the Woody Alan persona.

"Ladies and the one gentleman, I mean besides me of course, I welcome you again from the bottom of my heart and in all sincerity and blessings from my mother. I have one item to discuss with you all this evening." He nodded for Nurse Pickles to start the PowerPoint projector.

Potts used a green laser pointer. "Yes, my really good people, not only must you become accustomed to reading the nutritional ingredient list of a food package, but you must be aware of the amount of each one. That includes the grams of fat, protein, carbohydrate, and roughage."

"Next slide if you please, Mrs. Pickles. Yes, you see only one number on this slide…number six. You must always refrain from ingesting any food with a sugar content of greater than six grams. In the next slide you see the grams of sugar in a Milky Way® candy bar—29grams! For us that's poison."

Winnie was caught up in Potts' dialogue and words of wisdom. However, in the back of her mind was a sense of uneasiness. She kept looking around the room for a terrorist disguised as a nutrition student. The thought was as distracting as Potts' fluorescent hot pink necktie. She was also looking at the wall clock behind the podium. After the session she planned to talk to him about the NYPD and Father Nesbitt's warnings.

At the end of the class she waited in the short line. When she, Potts, and Pickles were alone she approached the podium.

Potts gave her his best Woody Alan numbness look. "Yes, my dear, dear Ms. Winnie, I trust you understood the importance of today's lecture?"

"Oh, yes, Dr. Potts, Your teaching ability is better than most of my acting professors."

Potts puffed himself out with over-stressed pride. "Thank you my dear. What might be your query tonight?"

"Well, I've already mentioned about the mugging I suffered in Central Park a few weeks ago." She looked from Potts to Pickles. Both suddenly became wide-eyed.

Pickles shut off the overhead projector, gathered Potts's notes and papers and started to leave.

Winnie grabbed Pickles' left arm. "Oh, no Mrs. Pickles, what I have to say is important for you also." Winnie began slowly and told of the admission of guilt by Flenk. She then segued into the reality of a terrorist stalker putting those around herself at possible risk.

"Terrorists!" Pickles dropped the papers to the floor and grabbed for the podium.

Potts immediately looked around the room buttoning his white lab coat. He jerked his head in all directions and went to lock the windows and doors. "Al Qaeda, here...in my suite! I'll not have it. They are not allowed in here." He pressed his green laser pointer and flashed it around the classroom. "Please, let's adjourn into my office."

Potts checked the locks on the office's windows and doors. He sat down and motioned Pickles and Winnie to sit in front of his desk. He folded his hands and leaned back in his squeaky chair. "My Dear Winnie, I'm very sorry about your circumstance. There is only one course of action for you regarding your ongoing treatment here." He paused and unconsciously pulled his hot pink tie out and held on to it with his right hand. "For the safety of my patients and staff, it will be necessary that you not attend any more office appointments or classes. Once this problem disappears, then you may resume your health program with us."

Winnie touched the arm of Pickles chair, "I expected this outcome, Dr. Potts. However, that still leaves you as a possible target for those who think you might know where I might be."

Potts pushed the back of his chair to the limit and fell totally backwards. The chair dumped him onto the floor. The action caused him to tighten his clutched pink tie around his neck. Potts shouted from the floor, "Help...I'm choking...I'm being garroted!"

Chapter 20
Monsignor Hannon

Father Nesbitt made a small 'to do' list after leaving Detective Bauman. He had thoroughly thought through the consequences of being put in harm's way by the current events. Nesbitt felt duty bound to inform the Monsignor and to protect Winifred Dorfinkle.

Monsignor Hannon listened silently to Nesbitt's words and responded with folded hands in low tones. "Forbish, wearing the uniform of the Lord as we do every day sets us up as fodder for all who feel that God has forsaken them." He unfolded his hands. "And, for those of other faiths, especially radical Islam, we are deemed infidels. We are to not only be shunned but terminated as well. We are easy to find. Any civilian who wears a crucifix is easy to find."

Nesbitt crossed his legs, "Monsignor, I know too well what it's like in the Middle East. The radical jihad extremists will even set off explosives in a movie theater or any gathering of people suspected of being non-Islamic. The worst is the group called ISIS. They kill even non-jihad Muslims." He uncrossed his legs, "But your holiness, I'm talking about my becoming a specific target. Al Qaeda thinks nothing of collateral damage with any effort to kill me."

Monsignor Hannon sat back. "You're going to tell me that it's possible for an entire congregation to be assaulted in an effort to get to you. You could be conducting a Sunday Mass, a well-attended marriage, or giving an opening prayer at a civil function."

"Exactly, what does the Vatican offer for such a predicament?" Nesbitt leaned forward.

"The Pope has protectors where he lives. His vehicle is bullet-proof. The Vatican has the ability to summon the Italian Army if necessary to protect its constituents." He stood up. "We, however, do not."

Nesbitt stood as Hannon moved around his desk. "I'm here to offer some possibilities."

"I'm all ears. I understand that there is no perfect plan, but go ahead."

Nesbitt faced Hannon, "The obvious is my isolation. If no one knows where I am, then I'm safe until the stalker is eliminated." He held up his hand to stop Hannon from responding. "This will only protect me, Father. It will also put all those who are in any way associated with me in danger. Terrorists will seek out such individuals. They'll use any means to extract information about my whereabouts. So here is what I propose." He paused as Hannon went back to his chair. Nesbitt sat down.

"All right Forbish, I'll listen and when you're done I'll offer my comments."

"NYPD has no spare bodies to offer as any kind of guardianship for me or the church. The US Navy cannot come to our aid in formal uniform or in any legal manner. Unofficially, however, I've been given a list of former Navy SEALs who have left the service for civilian life. They are available for spotting the jihadic trackers who are looking for me. The CIA will give us the information of the status of such terrorists. The plan will necessitate my staying here at St. Patricks. The SEALs will become part of St. Pat's constituents and only known to me and the staff here as newly to-be-ordained Priests. There will be SEALs at every mass and every church function. No St. Pat priest will be alone. A SEAL will be close enough to protect them —most even dressed in priestly frocks."

Hannon smiled, "Am I included as having a Navy man in attendance?"

"Yes, your holiness, however, no one other than you must know of this. The Vatican cannot be informed until this situation is neutralized."

"And how do I account for these soldier companions to the Priests they shadow, Father Nesbitt?"

"I will inform all of St. Pat's clergy that the guardians are potential proselytes, that they are under my responsibility for a new approach to encourage recruitment into the dwindling Priesthood ranks."

"So you relieve me of having to lie to anyone."

"It's better than the alternative. You know what the Vatican will say." Nesbitt stood up again.

"Yes, the Pontiff will say that we should do nothing. We will let God choose what shall happen." Hannon opened his palms and pushed them down on desk as he stood again. "Once this is over, it may mean you will be defrocked. The responsibility will be all on your shoulders. And this may happen even with a good outcome."

"I'm willing to take that risk. I left the Navy to leave the killing behind. But I now realize I may never be able to do this."

"Yours is the best proposal. I agree something must be done. I have one question for you."

"Yes, Monsignor."

"Did you ever go on any Navy SEAL operation wherein the Navy would disallow any knowledge of giving sanction to such action?"

"Yes...often."

"Then, my son, this will be such a situation. In my mind your operatives will be viewing for assessment of entering the Holy Order. They will be evaluating whether they should be following in your footsteps." Hannon shook Nesbitt's hand, "Father Nesbitt, I do hope God is with us on this. God bless your mission and I pray that our people are not harmed."

Chapter 21
Judge Dewey Deuser

Malcolm Flenk tightened his grip on the telephone receiver in the dimly lit jail's visiting hall. There were two rows of 20-foot-long tables partitioned into five open-top booths. A thick plexiglass separation enabled the prisoner and visitor to see each other. Each booth was separated from another by a thick soundproof covered partition. Communication was by a telephone. Flenk faced his lawyer, Rodney Ducette, and roared into the phone, "What do you mean, Judge Deuser won't be able to sit for my sentencing? We made a deal. You made the deal. I confessed, you prick."

Ducette pulled the phone receiver a few inches from his ear with Flenk's shouts. "It's out of our control, Malcolm. Deuser had a heart attack. The courts assigned another judge."

"Is this judge committed to honoring our deal?" Sweat beaded on Flenk's brow.

"I don't know. I'm meeting with Judge Roland Buttons right after I leave you."

Flenk wiped his face with his white jail-uniform sleeve, "What do you mean, You don't know? Our deal is a legal document isn't it?"

"Yes, and no, let me explain. The deal was for something other than a sentence of life imprisonment. We pled down to five years which means in three years you could get paroled for good behavior. A new judge has to honor the modification of a life sentence. He could give more or less." Ducette wiped his sweaty brow with a well-used used handkerchief.

"Less? I could get less?"

"It's possible." Ducette coughed and continued. "It could be the same or more."

Flenk was red-faced, "You better get me the same or less. I can't handle being locked up for life. I hold you responsible. If you don't get me what we bargained for, so help me I'll get out and kill you and those assholes I mugged. If I have to do life, I'll do it for murder...your murder and theirs."

Shahidi twisted around to look out the back window of Zamir's SUV. The Tappen Zee Bridge looked huge. "Ramik, we do not have such a bridge in my home in Iraq."

Zamir smiled, "There is not much need for bridges in our country. America has many bridges and most are larger than this. There are twenty-one bridges in and out of New York City."

Shahidi stared at the large lettering at the toll booth. "It cost money to use the bridge? Why is there only one side of the road for a toll booth? They do not charge money to leave the New York City?"

"That is correct. The bridge was built by New York City and the cost for using it is also for using New York City. The money helps pay for the bridge and its repair."

Shahidi looked into his wallet. "I think I know how to use the coins and the paper American dollars. I will be here only three days to look at the buildings. I have my interview at the International Imports building?"

"Yes, I will take you to your hotel and pick you up three days from now. We will then plan our attack." Zamir merged with the moving traffic. "The Wickman Hotel is only two blocks from the christian church where your Navy SEAL stays. You can see it from the hotel. Your tour tickets for the St. Patrick Church is for two days. Between tours you can go inside if you just sit on the praying bench."

"I will pray only to Allah, for the success of my mission." Shahidi frowned. "Will not my lack of Christian ways make me suspicious?"

"No, many visitors come just to take pictures or look at the inside. Some even enter to just get out of the weather." Zamir pulled into the main entrance for the Wickman.

"At our mosques we must pray. It would be an insult to Allah to just have selfish intentions for entering a holy place."

Zamir laughed, "That is why they are infidels. That is why our mission is holy. That is why we have selected the church for your action."

Attorney Ducette rose when Flenk was brought into the courtroom. Flenk's handcuffs and leg restrains were removed. The court officer called the court to order, "All rise for the Honorable Judge Roland Buttons."

Flenk whispered to Ducette, "Buttons? First Deuser and now Buttons, don't judges have normal names?"

"Quiet, we're first on today's docket." Ducette looked at his scruffy client. "Why didn't you wear the suit I picked out? You look like a street person."

"I'm not homeless. This is what I look like. I have a real address." Flenk scratched his developing red beard and his left chest.

Judge Buttons scanned the court attendees. He read from his first case file for the day. "The court will hear case number 24077, the State of New York verses Malcolm Phineas Flenk." The Judge banged his gavel for order at the laughter triggered by Flenk's name.

He read the list of accusations, "The charges are attempted aggravated robbery, possession of an illegal firearm, assault with a deadly weapon, and threat of bodily harm with threat of death." Buttons looked at the now standing Ducette and Flenk. "How do you plead, Mr. Flenk?"

Ducette answered for him, "He pleads guilty, your honor."

Buttons turned a severe look at them. "Such a plea spares the State of New York the expense of a jury trial. Considering the prior administrations with Judge Deuser and Attorney Ducette, this court can today present the penalties as prescribed by law."

Flenk inhaled loudly letting out an audible sigh. He clasped his sweaty hands together, looked at Ducette, and up at Judge Buttons.

"Although this is your third conviction, which ordinarily demands a lifetime of incarceration, this court will honor the plea bargaining efforts suggested by Judge Deuser." Buttons picked up a stapled collection of letter-size file pages. He cleared his throat and sipped from a glass of ice water. "For the charge of aggravated attempted robbery the court gives a sentence of five years."

Flenk and Ducette looked at each other with disdain.

Buttons continued, "For use of a lethal weapon in this felony another five years plus another five years for illegal possession of a firearm, second offense. For the charges of assault with intent to harm with stated possible lethal outcome, five years." Buttons paused and looked at them. "Mr. Flenk, you have also multiple charges of contempt of court secondary to initially denying guilt and falsely accusing two victims. This has done much harm to the revered institutions of Church and State. Another five year sentence is thus demanded."

Ducette raised his hand and started to speak.

"I am not through Counselor Ducette. The total sentence requires a penalty of servitude for twenty-five years. I point out that such sentencing honors the pre-court appearance agreement of deferring a life sentence.There are no financial penalties. Your behavior while paying your debt to society could reduce this term of incarceration. As of this moment you will be eligible for parole in fifteen years–earlier with good behavior. Now, I suggest that any further appeal be done by proper procedural channels. This case is closed. Next case."

Ducette grabbed Flenk's arm, "Keep your cool. We can appeal this."

Red-Faced Flenk clenched his teeth and glared at Ducette and the Judge. He said nothing. His thoughts, however, were like a volcanic eruption. *I'll be damned if I serve out a week. I know people. I can break out before they put me in prison. My connections in the City Jail will help.* He glared at Ducette with further thought, *I never told you of my Plan B. As soon as my sentence is publicized, my people will react.*

᛫

"There you go and welcome, Mr. Shahidi." The reception desk woman passed him his electronic key and his hotel welcome package.

Shahidi was amazed at how easy it was to move freely both in Europe and here in the United States. *The western countries call us terrorists but we are a Holy order—Allah's soldiers, Allah's Freedom Fighters. I feel totally committed to my cause, yet Americans do not see me as a threat. Why is this so? It is said by Nahlid that Americans classify all Islamics as terrorists, especially by the*

Donald Trump President. Yet when I declare my faith as being of Islam, I am welcomed.

He looked around at the people in the high-end Wickman hotel. *These infidels are totally ignorant of the words of Mohammad and teachings of Allah.* He looked at his plastic card key. Room 808, the eighth floor. The elevator indicated a total of thirty-four floors. Shahidi placed his small suitcase on the webbed valet and walked to the window. He looked at the total horizon with its many skyscrapers and focused on the large church. *St. Patricks is dwarfed and seems to be swallowed up by the cancerous capitalistic buildings. I look forward to tomorrow's tour which takes me to the replacement building for the twin towers Allah struck down on September 11, 2001.*

Chapter 22
Thespians

Winnie sat up front in the teaching classroom. She looked around the room. It seemed the other students also took a favorite seat whenever a didactic session was scheduled. The cross-talking disappeared as Professor Cornish Bangdot turned on the podium microphone.

He nodded to Winnie and spoke with his hands on his hips. His horsewhip pointer hung loose from his right wrist. "My fellow Thespians, the topic today is a favorite of mine and generated by a renown actor, also a favorite of mine—William Shakespeare. Consider the well-worn axiom: 'All the world's a stage and we are merely the players.' I am pleased to introduce a professional veteran actor and director, Jonathan Ralston."

Ralston seemed taller than Bangdot who was six-foot-two-inches. He held a tan cowboy hat in his right hand, which he waved to the audience. Ralston wore a royal-blue velvet sportcoat, a silver ascot, and indigo jeans over beige ostrich leather western boots. "Good morning ladies and gentlemen, I'm always pleased to address people who are sitting where I once sat. Most successful theatre people reach rewarding employment in acting from teaching institutions like this one."

Winnie loved to hear such words of encouragement. She remembered Ralston as primarily a hero figure in westerns, crime dramas, and political-war situational movies. *That was when I was a kid and teenager. He still looks somewhat like a cowboy with the hat, the boots, and the ascot.*

Ralston had a baritone voice with a slightly higher timbre than Father Nesbitt. He ran a finger down a left Elvis-type sideburn and threw Winnie a smile.

Winnie smiled back. *He must dye his hair black. Ralston must be at least 55-years old.*

"Professor Bangdot touched on my topic for you today with Shakespeare's words. We are all actors and actresses. That is to say, every man and woman on Earth are actors from birth to death. Consider what you were like before you enrolled in The Thespian Drama Academy."

Ralston put on his cowboy hat. "How many of you wanted to be a cowboy or a superhero in your pre-teen years." He looked down at Winnie again, "Or maybe as adolescents and definitely now that such dreams can be realized on the silver screen."

Winnie closed her eyes a few seconds, *father Nesbitt can be a hero one day and a saintly prelate the next. Yes, we are all actors and actresses.* She focused again on the speaker.

"The best acting comes out of learned experience. I don't mean experience like with hands on, although that helps. But it can come from reading a captivating novel or seeing something touching and memorable on the news." He paused to let the group reflect. "I'm thinking now of love scenes. Can you remember your first goodnight kiss? How about the terrifying experience of your driver's license test? Has not each of you fantasized about what it would be like to kiss someone, make love to someone, or actually be someone else?"

Winnie looked around the room at her classmates who, like she, nodded agreement.

"When we draw from those experiences and can incorporate them on stage or in front of a camera, it's called acting. For example, my best kissing scenes are those when I picture my co-star as my wife. I close my eyes, hold her in my arms, melt my lips onto hers. Such real life experiences can convert you into someone else. They can make your performance a mirror for the audience to do the same. Our job, and it is a means of employment, is to do the best we can from a printed script. If we can all recapture the feelings demanded of us as thespians from our real life situations, we will be doing just that."

Winnie began to think of her feelings recently. *Am I in love with Father Nesbitt? Do I experience fear for me, Dr. Potts, and Whitney Zotle? Do I generate anger for Malcolm Flenk?*

Flenk was furious. He knew he had to maintain control. Things were lax at the City Jail compared to his experience with state prison. Any outbreak or breach of behavior would tighten the guard on him. It would prevent success of his plan for escape.

It actually wasn't his plan. It was a design for breaking out of this lower security incarceration. His cellmate, Clement Bonzac, at Sing Sing, and he, discussed it many times. Bonzac, like Flenk, was a two-time loser. They were linked with similar attitudes about robbery, stealing, and low-grade petty crime. Flenk recalled their discussion when their prison terms were coming to an end.

"Malcolm, we have to prepare for avoiding repeat imprisonment in this State." Bonzac was built like a wrestler. He had bulked up with weight-lifting while at Sing Sing. Flenk was not inclined to fitness programs.

"You mean get a better lawyer if we get caught?"

"No Mal, I mean there's a weakness in the degree of security in the holding jails they put us in while we endure the DA's prosecution. I've worked out a way. It'll only be successful if we agree to help each other in the event we ever get caught again."

They had gone over the routine many times in prison and over the phone since they were both released. Bonzac handed Flenk a partially filled aspirin vial. "These pills aint aspirin. They're a short-acting benzodiazepine, like Valium®. You'll be unconscious for up to four hours. The jailer will have to call an ambulance. The first thing I'm goin to do when I get out is to convert a van into an emergency EMT vehicle."

Flenk had heard this so many times he really believed it would work. He let Bonzac continue as always.

"Keep these pills. I got them when I was working in the hospital infirmary. I have some of my own. They'll let you keep the vial since the label says it's only aspirin. The plan is that when we look like we're in a coma from an emotional collapse, they call for the EMT. Either you or me, whichever one of us it is, shows up with my EMT vehicle and emergency medical cart. It'll be our ride to a safe house. You'll wake up in five or six hours without any side effects."

"But Clem, how can we contact each other to get the ambulance?"

"We'll practice while were out and about. I already have a connection with a former inmate to several of the New York City holding jails. If you hear that I've been convicted, you automatically monitor the phone line and head for the jail in the ambulance. We'll have shut down receipt of the phone request by the legit EMTs. We then respond as soon as the jail issues the ambulance summons, and acknowledge that we're on the way."

Bonzac had been one of the phone calls Flenk was allowed by the City Jail. Flenk only had to say, "It looks like I got 25-years. I have a headache."

"Can you take an aspirin for it?" Bonzac had practiced this query as had Flenk.

"Yeah, I think I'll take it in four hours if the headache doesn't go away." The were the trigger words to activate their EMT ambulance.

So far, the only thing Shahidi didn't like was the food at the Wickman Hotel. He was astounded at the prices. Seven dollars for a four ounce glass of orange juice. A medium-size bowl of rice was nine dollars. He kept the "Do Not Disturb" sign on the outside doorknob as long as he was inside. His first day was passed in walking a three block radius from his hotel. The path included views of St. Patrick's from all sides. Only one of the high arch doors had an "open" sign and underneath the words "all souls welcome". Tomorrow, he would enter with other tourists. Zamir had provided a list of priests in attendance for the Catholic rituals.

Shahidi looked at the list and times for each prelate to officiate at some Christian rite. Of particular interest was the priest for the eleven o'clock Mass. The name of the priest was Father Forbish Nesbitt. However, in Shahidi's mind it transformed to Navy SEAL LCDR Forbish Nesbitt.

Chapter 23
The Infidels

It had taken only three days for Captain Delmore Craig to arrange for Nesbitt's former SEALs to arrive fully equipped to New York City. Nesbitt made the assignments for each SEAL and where they would be placed. He was grateful that the Navy had chosen only those men who had been in prior tactical missions with him.

Monsignor Hannon saw to the novice priesthood clothing for four of the SEALs. Nesbitt met with them in a small conference room off the left narthex. He addressed them each by first name.

"Nathan, Ron, Del, and Hal, it's good to see you all again. However, even in your saintly black novitiate priestly vestments you still look like combat-ready soldiers."

Harold (Hal) stood up, "And the same goes for you sir, or rather Father. We've been briefed on the do's and don'ts by Captain Craig and by Monsignor Hannon. We're ready to hear the mission, sir."

Nesbitt took a deep breath after a sip from his bottle of water. "Gentleman, please listen to the recap of my last combat experience and its consequences." He gave a detailed description of the deadly events in the small stone Iraqi house. "...and in summary only Omar Shahidi and I survived. Shahidi was actually a pacifist Islamic. His brother, Nabil, was the Jihadist who triggered the explosives.

That action, my friends, brought me to a search of peace by religion and not by guns. For Shahidi, however, his conversion is one of revenge and becoming an Islamic fascist like his brother. Captain Craig has briefed you all and me on Shahidi's training. We don't have everything about what he is, what he looks like now, or how he got into the US. We must be vigilant in our surveillance of all St. Patrick attendees."

Red-haired Ron raised his hand and spoke, "So we're focussing on St. Pats. What about out in the streets? What about this Winnie girl, that Doctor, and the girl's roommate? Omar might surely use them to get to us."

Nesbitt stood, turned his chair around and set his right foot on its seat, "The NYPD are only there for us when we call them. They're spread too thin to offer surveillance on Winnie, her roommate Whitney, or Dr. Potts." He held up his hand. "And we're also powerless over Winnie's classmates and teachers at the drama academy." He held up his palm again, "We do, however, have CIA agents who will keep track of them for us."

"What about the FBI? They sometimes help out the military. They helped us a few times…as Navy SEALS."

"Those two agencies are fierce competitors and get in each others way. Captain Craig favored the CIA. Besides the FBI and NYPD hate each other."

Nathan stood up, "Okay sir, but you've said nothing about this wild card crook who's a thorn in everyone's side on this. This slime ball Malcolm Flenk. He just escaped from jail. Do you think he'll be coming after you and Winnie?"

"I have photos of everyone we've mentioned, even a collective of Winnie's drama class including the professors. Yes, Flenk is a wild card. He faces a life sentence if he gets caught. If he's smart, he'll disappear forever. But I can tell you his brain is pure sociopathic criminal." Nesbitt smiled and picked up a file folder. "Right now you all have to be trained to be Catholic novitiates. And I want to introduce another vital member of our team. He can spot anyone who comes into St. Pats and will know immediately if he or she belongs here or not."

Nesbitt pointed at a shaded corner of the room. "Gentlemen, meet St. Patricks' most unfailing security system, Mr. Montague Kelp."

⌁

Two voices in the distance were speaking garbled words. Flenk's eyelids were as heavy as sewer covers. He tried to sit up but only his head responded.

Bonzac went over to him, "Easy, easy Mal, let the drug wear off. Take it slow. You're in the safe house—the one we rehearsed. Everything went according to plan."

⌁

Shahidi was in tour group number twenty-four. As far as he could tell he was the only Islamic. Almost all the women wore a crucifix. Most of the men were with the women as either spouse or friend. Two were students from a local college attending as part of a homework assignment.

He mingled with them and, although genuinely nervous about being in an infidel temple, he listened with fascination about who St. Patrick was, how the church came to be built, and its New York City status as a tourist landmark.

"These four small structures are St. Patrick's confessionals. You can see by the red light over each entry that they are occupied." The tour guide flashed a green laser pointer to the card on each stall indicating the name of the attendant priest.

Shahidi looked at each name and his eyes screeched to a halt on stall number three. *Father Forbish Nesbitt.* He felt his heartbeat hesitate and then speed up as an adrenalin rush took effect. He maneuvered his position closer to the pews opposite the confessionals. They were filled with people kneeling on tiny footrest-like boards. Some were clutching and moving different color beads. *A bomb detonated in a confessional could take out more than ten rows of these men, women, and children.*

Shahidi saw a man leave the last confessional carrying a business-like attache case. *Semtex filling that case would destroy Nesbitt and the entire middle section of the church with its infidels.*

Chapter 24
Montague Kelp

Kelp liked the SEALs. They were concrete thinkers and no nonsense "do it now" people like he was. He was baptized into the Catholic form of Christianity by virtue of his parents leaving him at the footsteps of the Home for Little Wanderers in the Bronx. The Home was run by a missionary component of St. Patricks. Children, including babies, who were not accepted into other orders because of social, mental, or physical defects ended up in the Home. Thus hunchbacks, frog-faced genetic throwbacks, kids with weird and scary voices, and those with obstinate, aggressive behavior became inhabitants of the Little Wanderers. His first name came from a Nun who was a Shakespeare fan. She selected a name from a Shakespearian play family line, the Montagues. His last name actually came with him as he was delivered in a fish-smelling little crate padded with ocean kelp.

He was nicknamed "the thing" by the Nuns and some of the older boys. As a child he was given labor intensive chores. His voice was a combination of gorilla grunts and shrill squeaks but his tonal result was a penetrating totally articulate dialect. He did well with school subjects, but was still shunned by his peers at the Home until he turned thirteen. By then his body was that of a mountain gorilla complete with a bony-prominent brow and downy facial hair. His muscles had over responded to his elevating hormones. Even at this early age he was the one called upon to move the Home's organ and piano. Along with voice and musculature changes came a name change. Anyone who called Kelp "the thing" or any other incongruent name ended up with a gorilla type knuckling to the top of their head. The nuns, staff, priests, and other kids now called him Monty.

His high school days at the Home were also worth mentioning. He was in the top five of his graduating class. Montague Kelp was indeed beloved by all, especially his adolescent peers. Monty was invited everywhere the orphans went. No one chided or derided them as "unfortunate, parentless waifs" with Monty around. Anyone who got physical with a Little Wanderer had their pugilistic assaults returned by Monty. Then time came for Monty to leave the home and make his way into the world.

Employment agencies would often engage Monty in the face-to-face interview process. Monty's voice and articulate conversations over the phone had job recruiters extending hopeful invitations for a personal meeting. It was his physical appearance of a cross between the "Creature from the Black Lagoon" and "Gorilla Monsoon" the wrestler that ruined it for him. Even the Army and Marines didn't want him to deface their image of handsome, athletic men in pristine uniforms. His big chance came when he enlisted in, and was accepted by, the US Navy. Kelp excelled in basic training and had no complaints about being classified for an aircraft carrier's engine room workforce. After two hitches in the Navy, Kelp found difficulty in mingling with the citizenry. His physical appearance negated positive acceptance in the public eye even with his Navy Honorable Discharge with meritorious service citations. Kelp turned to the church. It felt like a safe haven and as comfortable as the Home For little Wanderers. His job description was in reality a cross between janitor and sergeant-at-arms. He loved it, and now he was to interact with ex-Navy men. Kelp was excited and motivated.

Nesbitt introduced Kelp to his quartet of former combat-hardened friends. Kelp shook their hands with his right hand, while touching their biceps with his left. "Your arms are big like legs…like mine," Kelp grunted.

Nesbitt smiled with the rest of the group. "Okay guys, Monty will be keeping an eye on you. If he sees you doing something non-clergical, he'll appear and correct your situation. Are there any questions for Monty?"

Nathan was the only SEAL with a shaved head. He faced Kelp, "Yes, you sound like a good back-up person. How do we contact you?"

Kelp attempted a smile. His scraggly black beard was the result of lightly shaving only every fourteen days. The smile succeeded in giving him a face like that of an overgrown troll. "You all have one of these." Kelp held up a green cell phone. "I'm in the contact list as MK. If any of you want to talk to me for any reason just touch the 'MK' and say your name only. If you want me where you are and for any reason cannot speak, touch the MK and punch in your location. I know every inch of St. Patrick's and all the shortcuts to get anywhere fast."

Nesbitt acknowledged Ron the redhead, "Yes, Ron?"

"What's the range on these throwaway cell phones, Father?"

"I was getting to that. The green phones are for St. Patrick and its grounds. The camo phones are for use outside the St. Pat's buildings and grounds."

Navy SEAL Hal sporting a light brown crewcut was next, "What's our freedom of movement around New York City while on duty?"

"Each of you separately can go to Winnie's apartment building, the Drama Academy, and Dr. Myron Pott's office building. Your Big Apple world will consist only of those sites until the mission is completed."

Del (Delbert), the largest novitiate with a fullback's build, was next. "And can you please repeat this multifaceted mission again, sir?"

Nesbitt scanned the team including Kelp and responded, "Every AM and PM, which will be breakfast and dinner, I will be asking you as a group to repeat it. I want to hear the following from you: Number one is to keep an eye on me whenever possible. Shahidi and maybe another jihadist might be scoping me out as the main target. Second, these terrorists will most likely try to take out as many others, including me, as they can. So if you see me near a large crowd of St. Pat's constituents, be wary. Third, do not hesitate to contact Monty or any of us with any suspicion. Fourth, Winnie attends this church regularly, so keep an eye out for her. Fifth; remember, this is New York City and people like Malcom Flenk are everywhere. Try not to draw attention to yourself if approached by a mugger or any aggressor."

Nathan's hand shot up again, "What does that mean? What are our limitations?"

Nesbitt grinned, "You can't kill anyone unless it's unavoidable; you can't call the cops; or get into the news media."

Chapter 25
Winnie

Winnie loved the class and totally identified with Jonathon Ralston's concept that every human is born an actor or actress. Her cellphone vibrated as she crossed the street three blocks from the academy. Caller ID indicated it was from Father Nesbitt. Winnie's heart beat faster.

"Hello, Father. I just finished class. Is everything okay?" Winnie usually let the caller talk first. *I hope I'm not too anxious.*

"We need to meet today, now if possible. I need you to meet some people who will be looking out for us."

"Do you mean the police, Father."

"No, I'll explain when you arrive. Just come in the left door and Monty will take you to our meeting room."

"Who are these people, Father. Do I know them? I can't have strange men following me all over the City."

"No one will be breathing down your neck, even though they are like bodyguards. How soon can you get here?"

"I'm only a few blocks away, maybe twenty minutes."

"Good, see you then."

⤙

Clement Bonzac buttoned up his puffy car coat as the late afternoon chill arrived. He looked at his watch and then back at the front entrance of the Drama Academy. Finally, after waiting in the cold blowing air, he became alert as Winnie exited the building's main glass door. Bonzac looked at his watch and pressed a fast-dial button on his cell phone.

"Mal, Clem here, this actress babe is consistent. Her school gets out at three o'clock. This is the third time this week." Bonzac tugged his hood to hide his face as he began to follow her.

"Don't let her see you. Just keep track of when she visits that fucker Priest." Flenk clenched his left fist.

"She hasn't done that yet this week, Mal."

"If she goes to St. Patrick's, I want to know what entrance she goes in when she sees him. I doubt we can do anything inside the church sanctuary."

"I'll follow as far as I can without being seen."

"Clem, take photos with your cell phone, I'll need visuals for our plan. We have to figure the best place and time for them to be together. And don't forget, we need photos of the whole place and the grounds. They're vital for our exit strategy."

"Okay, okay, we've been over this a hundred times. I'll check back with you later." Bonzac pocketed his phone and continued his stalking. Winnie arrived at the church.

She went along the left side of the church on the four-foot wide concrete path to the two buildings in back. As she neared the first white clapboard structure where the clergy conducted private meetings in the small rooms, she stopped. Winnie looked at the church. St. Patrick's was built as a classical Catholic cathedral. The inside layout was in the shape of a cross. The area where the priest conducted services represented the arched top of the cross or apse. Right and left sections representing the cross contained open smaller chapel areas and enclosed rooms for private meetings. The open sections were where minor catholic ceremonies are performed for smaller group attendance such as a baby's baptism. Each apse could also have several rooms for private business, wedding instructions, or other ceremonial functions.

She stopped at the left entrance. *I feel like I'm being followed.* Winnie looked around. *Hmm, nobody there, or maybe it's Kelp skulking the grounds.* She went into the narthex or main church lobby and went directly up the left side aisle to the first room next to a smaller entrance/exit as Nesbitt had directed.

Winnie opened the door and went in. "Oh, I didn't know this was a private meeting." She looked at the new prelates at a round table and suddenly felt at ease. "Oh, Father Nesbitt, I don't want to interrupt your meeting. I'll come back later."

The group laughed. Nesbitt stood up, "Winnie this meeting is for you. I want you to meet the people who are going to be keeping a protective eye on both you and me."

The rest of the team stood. Winnie looked at the five people, all in priest black suits and white collar.

"Priests? It never crossed my mind that a priest could also be a bodyguard."

They laughed again. Nesbitt waved his hand to his comrades, "Let me introduce these four novitiate priests, who are also former Navy SEALs like me." Nesbitt made the introductions.

Winnie took a deep breath. *My God they're all such handsome, muscular men like Father Nesbitt.* "Well, I'm glad to meet you all and feel much relieved that you're here." She listened to their plan for their primary mission of focusing on she and Father Nesbitt.

"So, do you have any questions?" Nesbitt asked.

"Yes, I feel grateful about you guys here for me. But what about my Doctor—Dr. Potts, and my roommate Whitney Zotle?"

Chapter 26
The Guardians

A photo of Dr. Potts and Whitney Zotle was handed out to each pseudo-novitiate. Nesbitt held up Potts' picture. "Dr. Myron Potts is an addictionologist and nutrition specialist. The only reason we're concerned about him, Zotle, and the teachers at the Drama Academy is that they could be people of interest to our terrorists. Each one could be abducted to be forced into revealing the whereabouts of either Winnie or me."

Hal rubbed his chin, "Why Winnie or the others, sir? You're the only one the terrorist is after."

"He is after me, but remember he's now a trained Islamic extremist. Omar Shahidi will want to take as many non-Muslim lives along with mine. He can use Winnie to locate me. And that also means that he could use her roommate and Dr. Potts to find Winnie." Nesbitt looked at his SEAL team of priest-frocked combatants. "Any other questions?"

Nathan spoke, "Are you going to give them a heads-up that we might be stalking them?"

"No, Winnie will let them know the next time she sees her friends. She won't, however, be directly visiting anyone except Zotle, her roommate. She isn't going to inform her classmates or teachers. It might induce panic. And remember, above all, do not do anything that might end up on the Times' front page or TV screen news. We hope to keep collateral damage at a minimum if not zero."

"Okay let's go gentlemen," Del said. "We have a class on how to be priests."

The group left the room and exited the church by the left apse door. In a dark shadowed corner, a pair of watchful eyes followed the SEALs. After a minute the owner of the eyes followed them. He slipped into the room and pulled a chair into a dark corner. The man was quiet. Only one of SEAL pseudo-priest trainees designated for today's instruction nodded slightly to acknowledge Kelp's presence.

⤳

Hal ran his right hand through his crewcut hair. His assignment today after the didactic priestly pedagogue dismissed them was to scope out Dr. Potts. He adjusted his cold-weather black cloak and tilted his black wide-brimmed black hat to shade his face. Nesbitt advised tracking Pott's after at least a two hour wait parked at curbside outside Pott's office. His thoughts drifted back to Iraq and a briefing by his Team leader, LCDR Nesbitt.

"The Taliban often mingles with civilians. Taliban leaders can pass themselves off as Imams or holy Islamic priestly equivalents. The civilians will bow their heads at the real Imam but not the Taliban member. If at all possible do not take out a real Imam. If you do, we may not gain their confidence."

Hal switched to Nesbitt's words in today's briefing. "Our terrorist will not try to take me out if I'm alone. In fact, he won't try to take out any priest if they're alone. So, don't get into any crowd or group." Nesbitt paused. "There is one exception—Malcom Flenk, the guy who mugged us. I doubt he'll be after me and Winnie after his breakout from jail. Here's his picture. He walks slightly bent over and tends to tug at his flimsy beard. If you see him, don't hesitate to get him. Try to take him alive."

Flenk wanted Nesbitt and the girl dead. Revenge was a feeling nurtured in prison against that witch Domena. It was still driving him as a priority emotion. He looked at the clothes Clem Bonzac had got for him. A white embroidered skullcap, plain black shoes, and a full length black coat with buttons to the waist will transform him into a devout-appearing Muslim.

"Are you sure about that outfit, Mal." Bonzac smiled. "I mean you could be taken for a terrorist."

"Never, with this outfit people may look at me, but all they'll see is an Islamic American carrying a book—the Koran. I'll put a camera around my neck and blend in with other tourists. I just have to know when both Nesbitt and the girl are together." Flenk rubbed his now clean-shaven face and held up a camera by its long straps. "That's why it's so important you keep tracking them. This St. Patrick tour ticket you got me is good for any day of the week."

A hairy hand grabbed Nathan's right shoulder. Nathan turned quickly ready to grab and immobilize his assailant. He turned slightly and grabbed a hair-covered wrist. One twist and the man's forearm bones would both be broken.

Suddenly, his legs were kicked out from under him. A raspy voice looked down at him. "I didn't mean to startle you. Let me help you up."

"Mr. Kelp, where did you learn that maneuver?" He gripped Kelp's offered arm and stood beside him.

"Same place as you. I did some training in the Navy for Special Operations. I'm sorry, I should have spoken first. I forgot who my friends are."

"What's that you have in your hand?"

"An envelope with pictures of someone who was stalking Winnie Dorfinkle today." He pulled a photo from the envelope. "This man waited outside the apse wing for her to leave. He didn't follow her after this."

Nathan looked at the picture. "Who is this? I thought we had the photos of everyone we're supposed to keep and eye out for."

"I don't know. I used my phone-camera and printed out the picture." Kelp handed him the envelope. "Give them to Father Nesbitt and your team members. Father Nesbitt may be able to find out who he is."

Nathan looked again at the picture of a man with an unshaven face and long salt and pepper hair. He traced a scar on Bonzac's right cheek. "Yes, thank you. I'll give it to him right now."

Chapter 27
Empire State

Shahidi mingled with the crowd. He was grateful that Zamir had given him a heavy knee-length puffy coat and fur-lined gloves It was a brisk fall day with a biting cold wind. The tour guide was also bundled up.

"Ladies and gentlemen, it feels cold now at ground level, but it's going to be much colder when we reach the top of the Empire State Building. Although there is a heated gift shop and a less-heated glass-enclosed section for photo opportunities, I suggest that those of you without winter clothes stay behind or visit the gift shop only. When we leave the elevator at the top please stay with our group. There will be other groups, so please stay together." The tour guide looked at his small crowd.

A few women and young men in light clothes and T-shirts moaned disappointed sounds and left. The tour man motioned the rest to the multi-elevator lobby and made one more announcement, "Everyone must go through the metal detector. Ladies please place your handbags in the trays for the x-ray device. Other metal items like keys, coins, and belts with buckles must also go into a tray. Wrist watches are okay."

Shahidi stared at the two security positions. *Ah, Zamir was right. It is good I have no weapons until the day of our plan.*

"Please swallow as you hear your ears 'pop' with the change in altitude," the guide advised.

It is like on the airplane, Shahidi mused. The large elevator also held another tour group. He looked at their larger numbers. Two were in Middle Eastern clothing, one man and one woman. They were holding hands. *They must be married.* Their group leader raised a yellow umbrella. Shahidi's guide raised a blank blue placard. Each group was to remain close to their respective tour guide holding up their identifying color. The elevator stopped and a blast of icy wind offered resistance to an otherwise easy exit.

Shahidi looked around. There were other people and other groups listening to their tour directors. His guide summoned the tourists around his blue guidon. "The first thing you will notice beside the wind and colder temperature is the barred metal fence surrounding the perimeter at our level. The pointed tops of each bar is curved inward to prevent people from climbing higher. This is not so much to stop people from getting a better view, but rather to stop disturbed individuals from jumping to their death—suicide."

Suicide to no purpose other than self reasons is an affront to Allah. There would be no entry into Paradise for just leaping off this place. Shahidi looked around and started to count the numbers of tourists on their side of the building. *Almost sixty people. It would be a good place to*

detonate an explosive-vest and destroy these non-believers.
He listened again to the guide's dialogue.

"Ladies and gentlemen, if it gets too cold while you
are enjoying the view and taking pictures, please go inside
to the gift shop or elevator lobby. We will be going next to
an enclosed floor with large clear windows where it'll be
warmer and free of the wind. Please follow me while we
move to each side of the Empire State Building, which was,
in the 1930s, once the tallest structure in the world."

The two Muslims from the other group moved in-
side to the elevator lobby. *This is my opportunity to talk to
another Islamic.* Although he was dressed in American
style clothes to blend in, he did want to experience the feelings of these people. He spoke to them in Farsi, "What
country are you from? Why are you here in the United
States?"

The Muslim man's eyes widened as he returned
Shahidi's questions with his own queries, "Why do you not
speak English? We are Americans. Where are you from?"

Shahidi apologized. He had just done what he was
not supposed to do—draw attention to himself. "I beg your
pardon." Shahidi's English had less accent than the tourist.
"I come from London, England. I am an interpreter, just in
the US a few days only."

The woman pulled her scarf over her lower face and
remained silent. The man spoke again, "We are from Arizona—out west in the United States. We are visiting relatives who are also American citizens like us."

Shahidi was puzzled, "But you dress like in our countries. I am originally from Iraq. I speak and dress similar to the country I work in."

The man and women seemed to visibly relax. The man nodded to his mate, "We have lived in this country fifteen years. There are many like us as you will find out in your job in New York."

"But are not Americans distant toward Islamics? Did you have to give up your allegiance to your country?" Shahidi was still confused as to how easy it had been to enter this country and mingle within its population.

The man smiled and answered, "No, we are from Iran. Our families and we, also came here where being a citizen and believing in Allah at the same time does not provoke punishment. Our children were born here and they are citizens."

"But Americans send soldiers to my Iraqi village and other neighbor states. They use bombs and guns against us. Why don't they do this here?" This was a feeler question. *I must understand how Americans allow Islamics here without imprisonment or detainment.*

"Islam extremists attacked New York City and destroyed two tall buildings such as this. They killed thousands. It is written in the first book of Koran to be peaceful not warlike to fellow Islamics and those of other faiths. We in the United States punish only those who attack its citizens. They are called Al Qaeda, Taliban, and ISIS as you must know."

Shahidi nodded agreement, "Yes, yes, I understand that. In my work as interpreter I must work with those who prefer peace."

The woman nudged her husband and whispered into his ear, "Our tour guide comes. We must leave this person."

"Excuse me, we must rejoin our tour. We go to the warmer floor to take our pictures. May I take yours?"

"No, it is okay. I also must join my group." Shahidi made and abrupt exit.

The two Muslims stared after him. The man spoke, "Allah be praised, I do not understand that someone comes to this country without knowing it protects its people from harm and allows all religions."

The woman spoke for the first time, "I agree. He seems to see life as one from the old country."

"It is too bad we did not get his name or his picture. He could be one of those who are the reason we came to America to avoid."

The woman pulled her scarf down and from under her blanket-like floor-length coat she turned her cell phone screen toward him. "I took these photos while you talked with him."

Shahidi looked out over the vista of skyscrapers and the seemingly endless scape of houses. He marveled at the number of bridges with slow-moving cars going in either direction. *My mission is to strike our enemies before they*

*strike us. I do not know why that man did not understand
this. He has lived here fifteen years and yet still wears the
garments of the Islamic faith. I am here three days and was
trained to blend in with American style clothes.*

His tour guide pushed the elevator button to the enclosed floor in the Empire State Building for the more sub-
dued, warm, and enclosed views. Shahidi looked for the
two people he had talked with and saw the yellow umbrella
raised high for their group. They were taking pictures. *It is
good I did not tell my name or place of address to them.*

Suddenly a thought flashed as he watched them take
pictures of each other. *Did they or someone else take a picture of me?*

The two tours descended to the lobby again in the
same elevator. Shahidi watched the two Islamics enter the
gift shop. He made his move toward them.

"Hello, again, I saw earlier you were taking pictures
of each other. Would you like if I took a picture of both of
you together?"

The man smiled, "I should have thought of this
when we were on top. But thank you, if you would be so
kind." He handed his phone to him.

Shahidi delayed finding them an agreeable back-
drop for the photo. While they were looking away, he
scanned their cell phone to see if they had taken his picture.
He could find no photo of him either single or with a group.

Shahidi took several photo's of the couple and returned their camera. He took a few with his camera.

"Would you like me to take one of you on your phone…we don't know your name."

Shahidi had a thought, "No thank you. Here is my card with my London address. I don't have one for here yet."

The man opened his wallet and pulled out a business card. "And here is mine with my name, Adem Saleem, and our Arizona address."

Shahidi maintained three business cards with false names. He bid them farewell.

The woman watched Shahidi leave. She turned to her husband, "I am afraid about this man. I saw him scanning the photos on your cell phone." She took out her phone, "I still have his photo on my cell phone and I think we should show it to someone."

"No, no, it is okay. He was just being friendly taking our picture." He looked again at the departing Shahidi. "Did you really see him looking at my recent pictures?"

Chapter 28
Father Nathan

Nesbitt motioned Nathan to his side. "It's your turn to get a first hand look at Winnie and this doctor…Dr. Potts. Use your GPS to find Winnie, I have her cell phone set for tracking. Here's her number. Meet with Winnie first. As for Potts, he and his nurse usually leave the office together."

Nathan wore his long black coat over his priestly black suit. His head was covered with a black watch cap and a long triple-wrapped black wool scarf was around his neck. He pulled it up to protect his face and nose from the cold. Nathan waited patiently just inside the doorway of the Drama Academy.

Malcolm Flenk resented the long cold trek following Father Nesbitt from St. Patricks. He was gambling that the Priest would be rendezviewing with the girl. *Maybe it's not so much a gamble, according to Bonzac. The girl usually leaves by three o'clock. What's her name, Winnie something? Damn, the only thing I can think of is Winnie the Pooh. My right arm is cramping with cold and holding this AR-16 under my coat.*

The sidewalks were filled with people going in either direction. Flenk moved with his left side forward into the wind to avoid bumping the hidden rifle into people. After thirty-five minutes the cramp in his right shoulder was starting to throb. *Hell, I might not be able to shoot accurately even with the scope-sight if my arm and hand get spasmed up. I'll give it another fifteen minutes before I quit.*

Flenk finally stopped his stalking and began massaging his arm with his gloved left hand. *Why am I so cursed with bad luck?* He watched the Priest wait at the pedestrian crossing light. The light changed and the "Walk" sign came on. Flenk let his eyes follow the black-frocked target. *Wait, he's stopped in front of this building. It's the Thespian Drama Academy! Nesbitt is going to meet with the girl.*

He continued to move his right arm with elbow and wrist flexing-extension movements. *Ah, the cramp's letting up. I'll wait until he goes through the doors and choose my best position for when they come out.*

⤴

Nathan was grateful for the warm foyer inside the Academy entrance. He looked at his watch. It had taken him almost forty-minutes to get here moving against the cold wind. As he was deciding on how much more time to linger for her exit, Nathan heard a loud eager voice.

"Father Nesbitt, Father Nesbitt, over here." Winnie couldn't see Nathan's face. She waved and called again.

Nathan responded with a return wave.

She rushed up to him and gave him a hug. "Oh, dear," she whispered. "Your not Father Nesbitt, you're one of the new priests. I mean one of the practicing priests. No, I mean you're one of the Navy guys pretending to be priests. Oh, you know what I mean."

"Yes, I know what you mean. Thanks for the nice greeting. I appreciate the warm hug."

Winnie blushed, "I'm sorry. I mean, I'm not sorry, just sort of embarrassed I got the wrong priest. I mean, I don't usually hug just any priest. I mean I don't usually hug Father Nesbitt. It's just, you know, I'm just so grateful for feeling protected."

Nathan smiled, "It's all right, I understand. We wanted to get you used to one of us letting you know we're around. After we learn your routine, we'll melt into the background. Anytime you plan to leave your apartment or the Academy send a message from your phone. One of us will be mobilized. Most important is your signal to us that you'll be heading for St. Patricks. You'll need a guard whenever you enter the church."

She buttoned up her heavy coat and wrapped her scarf from her neck to her nose. "I'm following your example, Father Nathan. Part of the reason I didn't recognize you was half your face was covered."

"Believe me you need to bundle up today." Nathan resumed his wintry garment adjustment. "You're heading for home now, so let's go."

"I thought Father Nesbitt was going to walk me to my apartment," disappointment was in her tone.

"Father Nesbitt still has his Catholic duties to per-form. He'll call you later."

Winnie tucked her right arm through Nathan's bent elbow as they moved to the doorway.

◄

Flenk prayed for a means of partial concealment to raise his blanket-covered rifle. He found a spot at the rear of a double-parked UPS delivery truck that was perfect. The truck was empty and the driver had just disappeared into a skyscraper with an over-loaded dolly with at least two dozen packages. He rested the blanketed rifle on a rear hinge of the truck's door, which was at collarbone level. *Resting the barrel of the rifle will take the spasm out of my cramped arm. I can use my trigger finger now. Okay you two bastards, come on out.*

He looked through the scope as it covertly emerged from the ruffled blanket. To passers-by, no part of the weapon could be seen. In fact, it appeared to Flenk that no one even gave his presence a glance. New Yorkers seem to walk like zombies, wrapped up in their own private world. The two large doors appeared so clear, he felt he could reach out and touch them. *They'll be coming out the right door since people are entering the left one.* Flenk reached out to check on the tightness of the three-inch suppressor at the tip of the barrel. *The background noise of the streets and sidewalks should add to completely wiping out the sound of the shots. The only sound will be the bullet reach-ing the sound barrier after it leaves the barrel. Anyone hearing the shot will not be directed at me but at the target. I can't do anything about the puffs of smoke.*

✤

Nathan and Winnie reached the door to exit on their right. It would be the left door for Flenk's shot. He held the rifle tight on the UPS truck's rear door hinge. The left side of the truck was blocking the wind. The Academy door opened slowly as the blowing winter current tried to counter the exit effort.

Nathan was in front of Winnie. Nathan suddenly was thrown back into the foyer landing on top of Winnie. "Stay down. I think I've been shot."

Winnie lay on the floor staring at Nathan. "I don't see any blood. Do you hurt anywhere?"

Nathan reached down with his left hand touching his left thigh. "I feel pain in my chest and left leg."

Blood was now discoloring the lower left side of Nathan's long coat. "Unbutton my coat and use my scarf as a tourniquet for my leg. Use the large cross I'm wearing to tighten the tourniquet."

"Oh my God, I've never seen so much blood. It's so dark." Winnie wrapped the scarf around the upper leg and twisted the cross to tighten the loop. The dark maroon blood stopped flowing. "What about your chest, Nathan?" She felt the front of his sternal area. "There's a small tear but no blood."

"We're all wearing bullet-proof vests. There shouldn't be any penetration in the chest. But, damn, it hurts like hell."

I know I got Nesbitt right in the chest. My second shot should have done the same with the girl. Flenk couldn't check on the accuracy of his shots. People were crowding on both sides of the Academy doorways. He looked around. *No one's looking my way. I hope I got them both, but at least my shot was right on with the Priest.*

Chapter 29

The Thespian Drama Academy

Nesbitt and Hal went as fast as they could to Columbia Presbyterian Hospital. Nathan was being readied for surgery.

"I'm Dr. Portman, General Surgeon on call today. I'm handling all trauma and triaging all ER surgical candidate patients. The bullet was a .223 calibre. It missed the bone but tore a branch of the femoral vein, Father."

Nesbitt looked down at Nathan who was now sedated prior to the trip to the OR. "Tell me in English what it means, Dr. Portman."

"First, the protective vest saved a bullet from a dead-on heart trajectory. The leg bone was spared so there'll be no problem with Father Nathan's ability to walk. I do have to explore the wound to determine how much blood vessel repair is needed. He may need some blood but the lab work will tell us that. We're taking him to surgery now."

"Is it okay to wait around until you're finished—for a final assessment I mean." Nesbitt held Winnie's hand in his.

Portman smiled, "I'm afraid you have no choice. As the responsible person, the police want to talk to you. All bullet wounds get their attention by law. Secondly, and you may have to dodge this group, is the press. Shooting a priest rates front page news next to shooting a cop."

Nesbitt wasn't happy about hearing the press might be looking for him about the attempted assassinations. He turned to Hal. "I certainly was the target in this. I'm concerned about the second shot. It was low and got Nathan's leg. What are your thoughts Hal?"

Hal looked at Winnie before answering. "Winnie could you tell which bullet came first?"

Winnie looked from Hal to Nesbitt and back to Hal. "Yes, the chest wound happened first and then the leg almost right after. Why do you ask?"

Hal turned to Nesbitt, "You're right in your thinking, sir. Whoever did the shooting was after both Nathan and Winnie. The second shot was meant for the shorter target. The first round hit and turned Nathan. Nathan's body was moved to cover Winnie and he took the second shot, meant for her, in his leg." Hal looked at Winnie's puzzled expression.

"Hal, it means the shooter wanted to kill both me and Winnie. In this case he mistook Nathan for me. It also means that the shooter most likely was not Omar Shahidi. Shahidi was trained by either Al Qaeda or the Taliban. They don't like to single out one person. Typically they would rather kill their selected target in a crowd and they would use explosives rather than a bullet or use both." Nesbitt put his arm around Winnie. "Winnie, it looks like we have two separate and probably unrelated assassins out to get us."

Winnie covered her mouth as she spoke, "But the Iraqi you told me about has a priority of avenging his family. He would have no reason to single me out."

"Right Winnie, Can you think of anyone in New York City who hates the two of us enough to have done this shooting?"

"Oh, Father Nesbitt, I've never made any enemies ever in my life. In fact, the only person whoever threatened my life was..." She lowered her hand from her face and grabbed Nesbbit's coat sleeve.

Nesbitt nodded in agreement, "Yes, Malcolm Flenk." *We'll need more than the power of prayer now that we have enemies on two fronts—Flenk and Shahidi. I fear only for Winnie. What does that mean? I keep thinking about my life being empty without her.*

Hal reflexly looked around the ER waiting room, "Sir, do you think we should be armed?"

Nesbitt sighed, "We have no choice. However, it was a good thing Nathan wasn't carrying a weapon or this incident would have generated publicity that would bring in not only the NYPD in force, but the FBI and CIA. There might even have been panic in the streets."

"Sir, the four of us have access to Beretta 9 mms," Hal whispered.

"I have my own, Hal."

Shahidi and Zamir stared at the New York Times front page article about Father Nathan being shot at the

Drama Academy. Zamir commented first, "No one of our cell would have done such an act. This incident could jeopardize our mission."

"Tell me again about this girl." Shahidi pushed back on the parlor chair at their Suffern safe house.

"I have saved the newspapers that have made publish of this. A man who is called a mugger attempted to steal money from Nesbitt and this girl as they walked in the Central Park." Zamir paused as Shahidi scanned the separate newspaper issues. "This man, this Malcolm Flenk, is a lower thief who used a pistol to do his act. He was arrested and was supposed to go to prison."

Shahidi wrinkled his brow, "Are you saying this ... Flenk...is not a locked-up prisoner?"

"This last paper tells of Flenk fleeing jail. It was thought he has disappeared to a far away place. It looks like he, too, wants revenge against Nesbitt and also this girl."

"What shall we do?" Shahidi stood and paced once around the room. "Wait...our plan can still work if the Flenk man is eliminated."

"Yes, but how are we to find him. We must act now on Nesbitt. We can still get him in the church of St. Patrick when they have one of those Mass prayer meetings." Zamir picked up the phone. "I must discuss this with our region manager."

٭

Flenk moved rapidly out of sight after firing the two shots. No one seemed to notice. He moved to the sidewalk where the UPS truck hid him and moved away from the scene. He walked at a fast pace with the rifle still tightly clutched beneath his long coat. Those on the sidewalk were now looking behind him toward the sound of sirens. He stopped and looked with them to avoid suspicion. *All New Yorkers are rubberneckers. If I don't turn to look, I'll stand out in the crowd.*

He reached his old Ford SUV and placed the blanket-wrapped rifle on the floor behind the driver's seat. Flenk slapped the steering wheel with his exuberance. He spoke to his streaked windshield, "I did it. I got them both. I can hardly wait for the New York Times to tell the world. Then I can head for California."

Chapter 30
The New York Times

Dr. Myron Potts, the addictionologist, had only one addiction, the morning New York Times. His wife set out his 400 calorie healthcare breakfast right out of his office practice syllabus of foods designed not to kill you. One of the headline sections stopped his fork of non-yolk scrambled egg in mid trajectory to his open mouth. "Thespian Drama Academy student!" He hurried through the front page and turned onto the referred interior page to complete the write-up.

Potts' wife Zeldina stared at him as he completed the article and gazed up at her. "What's the matter? Is something wrong with your food?"

"No...it's...it's the news. I think one of my patients was shot yesterday. His brow was sweating. If it was her, I may or not be in danger. I mean we may be in danger. The woman survived and is being held in a safe house for protection. If she's my patient, the shooter may come after me...us...to try to find her."

Zeldina clutched her hand to her breastbone, "Do you know where she might be?"

"She gave an emergency address on her initial patient application questionnaire. Oh, my God dear, what shall I do?"

Monsignor Hannon studied the New York Times article and looked up at Father Nesbitt. "The paper doesn't mention the girls name or where she's hiding. Father Nesbitt, I'm only allowing her to live in the Nun's rookery here because of my original commitment, which was sanctioned by the Cardinal. You do have three other ex-Navy SEALs in good health staying here, so I task you with the safety of our staff and supplicants."

"Monsignor, the media did not tell of where Nathan was working. St. Patrick's was not mentioned per order of the NYPD and FBI. If there is any indication or imminent threat to anyone at this Parrish, then all of us will move to a safe house."

Hannon stood up, "But if you do that St. Patricks will be in the news. Word will spread fast and no one will be visiting our pews. My God Nesbitt, Thanksgiving and Christmas are fast coming upon us."

"Yes, it will be safer for us to all stay here, your holiness. Whoever is after me and the girl has lost the opportunity of going back to the Drama school. The NYPD has it under 24-hour surveillance. My three SEALs in priestly disguise, plus me and Kelp as a constant lookout, will give us ample warning of any evil presence."

"You're only four people—five, counting Montague Kelp."

Nesbitt leaned forward and lowered his voice, "There are aways to be others from the Navy mixed in with the congregation. Your eminence, I need your help also."

"What? What more can I do beside giving shelter, prayer, and assisting with dressing up your Navy men like proselyte priests?"

"I need you to have everyone who enters St. Patricks sign in. I'll supply the equipment."

Hannon's eyes widened, "What equipment?"

"I'm having three laptop computers scanning each frontal entrance. Every person or spokesperson for a group, like a family for example, will type in their names. The computer will match them with those of St. Patrick's sub-scribed members. It will automatically tell us who to look at those who do not usually come here." Nesbitt crossed his fingers.

"We already do that with tour groups." Hannon sighed. "Okay, but I can't spare any priest to standby a door and babysit the computers."

Nesbitt smiled, "I have other men to do this. The computers are linked to my men's smart phones. They'll come immediately to the door when the laptop entry sends an alert."

"There might be a few false alarms."

"Not many, I hope."

Hannon threw up his arms, "Okay, okay, but I have a bad feeling about this."

᠕

"Oh, piss, shit, dammit!" Flenk stood up and hand-ed the Times to Bonzac. "I got the wrong priest and missed the woman. Fuck!" He sat down and stretched his arms out on the sofa.

Bonzac read silently and looked up at Flenk, "The Priest was shot in the chest and the left leg. He survived. How the hell did you aim at the wrong man?"

"Look at the picture. The Priest had a scarf wrapped up to his eyes. It was so damned cold out his face was covered. We need another plan." Flenk stood and paced around the small living room. "The NYPD says, according to the Times, the acting-school is going to be under 24-hour police protection."

Bonzac rubbed his stubbled chin, "I need to follow her again. One thing's for sure, that Nesbitt Priest will probably never leave the church. The NYPD ain't goin to be there neither. The Times says the acting student, the girl, will still be attending class. That's crazy, it leaves her wide open for another shot." He turned to the inside of the continued front-page Times report. "Oh wait, she'll be taken there by NYPD patrol car."

Flenk brightened, "That means they'll be picking her up and taking her somewhere...but where."

Bonzac bought into the thinking, "Right, we may not know the pickup place, but we can follow them when they bring her back."

↜

The phone sounded three rings and then stopped. Shahidi and Zamir stared at the phone. It rang three more times and stopped again. Zamir held up his hand and extended his fingers. "If next it rings five times we pick up." The phone rang five times and Zamir immediately picked up the receiver.

Zamir looked at Shahidi as he listened and spoke slowly, "And unto you peace. Allah is with us." Zamir went silent again and looked again at Shahidi. He covered the phones mouthpiece. "Omar, I am getting instruction on the American criminal." Zamir listened and spoke a disconnect offering to Allah. "May Allah be with you."

"Well, what is to happen?" Shahidi asked.

"We are to focus on the Priest Navy SEAL Nesbitt only. Another cell will deal with the criminal person to avoid further distraction."

Chapter 31
The Nun

"I feel so excited. Wait until the others at the Academy see me in this. It's real life acting." Winnie adjusted her flowing nun habit. It was all black except for the white headpiece, which reached her shoulders.

Nesbitt laughed. They were in the small lobby of the Nun's Quarters. "You're only to go to-and-from the Drama School, Winnie."

"Oh, and Father look at this." She lifted up her ankle-length black skirt. "See, baggy pants...black culotte pants. I always wondered what nuns wore underneath. They let me wear my own underwear though."

He looked around avoiding her gaze.

"Why Father Nesbitt, you're blushing."

"Winnie, what if someone sees us and you're doing this. I mean, it could be misinterpreted as a sexual advance." Nesbitt motioned Winnie to lower her skirts.

"Oh, I'm sorry Father. I wasn't thinking of that. I mean I probably am now that you mentioned it. I mean what if a nun wanted to have sex. I mean all the layers of clothes. It would destroy the heat of the moment, wouldn't it, Father?"

Nesbitt's slightly reddened face couldn't help retain a hint of a grin. "Nun's don't think of having sex. Their outfits are designed not to stimulate such thoughts."

Winnie reached out and touched Nesbitt's hand, "If we had sex, would you think you would be violating a nun? I mean don't you think I'm a good actress?"

"Winnie! You are not a nun."

"So if we had sex it would be a romantic thing, Father. Oh Father I think of us in that way sometimes—like now." She threw her arms around his neck and kissed him.

Nesbitt put his hands on her shoulders. He did not push her away.

She kept her embrace and looked up at him. "Oh, Father Nesbitt, I know you're a priest but, you're also a man. Don't you ever have doubts that being a priest was a direction you maybe shouldn't have made?"

He slowly moved her back. "I do think exactly that, but not for the romantic possibilities. I chose the clergy to live and profess peace. And what happens to me? I get thrown into a world of violence that I thought I left behind in the Navy." *I also have feelings for you, Winnie, that are human, that go beyond my supposed calling for the church.*

She held his hand, "You've been tested by God and received his answer. Father, you are needed as the sword of the people just like some of the angels in the bible."

There was a knock on the windowless door.

"It's the patrol car to take you to school, Winnie. You'd better go." He squeezed her hand. "And be careful. Never be alone. When school is out, please wait for the police to pick you up." He let go of her.

"Oh, Father, you kissed me back. I could feel it." Winnie adjusted her habit and tied a bow at the neck of the heavy black woolen cloak. She turned to him as she left with a framed glowing face and smile, "And think Father, all this has happened because I dreamt I had sex with a banana."

Nesbitt rolled his eyes, "Winnie, what has transpired is from our being mugged in Central Park and an event from my deployment as a Navy SEAL in Iraq. Now off you go."

He watched her twirling around before entering the police car and waving to him. He suddenly felt that he should be going with her—to protect her. Nesbitt reflected on their kiss. *My God, I did kiss her back...and it was wonderful.*

᛭

Bonzac sat at the wheel of the old SUV. Flenk scanned the church with his mini-binoculars. "Mal, you see anything yet?"

Flenk smiled, "Yeah, a cop car pulled into the St. Pats driveway around back."

"Do ya see the Priest or the girl?" Bonzac twisted his body to try to get a view. "I can't see nuthin."

"Here comes the cop car. There are two cops in front. Wait, they're gonna go right past us." Flenk adjusted the focus. "There's just a nun in the car. Why the hell would a cop car pick up a nun?"

Bonzac stared at Flenk, "C'mon lets follow them. I think the nun might be our girl."

They stayed three cars behind the police vehicle. Traffic moved at its usual New York City pace—slow. Bonzac banged on the steering wheel and threw Flenk a glance. "I'm thinking it might be tough to kill the girl and get away in this snail pace traffic."

Flenk scratched his stubbly face, "I'm worried about those two cops. How're we going to get the girl? And then we gotta figure on how to get the priest."

"Ha, ha, the Priest is easy. We go to church and get'm in confession."

Flenk didn't laugh. "Confession, I ain't been in church since the sixth grade."

Bonzac looked at the traffic starting to thin out a little. "Ya know, we really are just followin them to see if we can get the priest and girl together."

Flenk fingered the binocular straps around his neck, "If the nun is the girl, then the cop car will take her back to the church. I bet they's goin right to the acting school where I shot the wrong priest."

"Okay, that makes sense. Our plan's gonna be to just follow the cop car. If the car dumps her at the school then we know it's her dressed up as a nun." Bonzac burped. "I'm gettin hungry. We shoulda brought sandwiches or somethin."

An older Winnebago was also in traffic two cars behind Bonzac's SUV. The driver slid open a small window to talk to his passenger in the cabin sleep area over the roof of the driving space. "Can you see good up there?"

"This camp truck it is high enough. I can see over all cars. The car we follow also follows the police one." A man in dirty, stained camo fatigues and a black watch cap looked out of the camper from the bunk overlying the top of the Winnebago's driving seat.

The Winnebago driver moved his hand over his tan Islamic skull cap. "Did you check on the window in front of your position?"

"I check it before we left. I check it when we were at the infidel church." The camo man slid a long RPG-weapon from a waterproof zippered covering.

The skull cap driver looked around, "I do not see parking spaces anywhere and they are slowing down. The police car turns on its colored top lights. They are stopping. The car behind also stops behind the police. A covered church-woman is getting out and a policeman walks with her to inside."

"I see this. The girl is gone inside building. The police are leaving. The following car is parking in fire-marked zone illegally and facing forward against the traffic. What is it we must do?" The camo man jerked his head from side-to-side. "We cannot stop here. We must turn around and keep coming back until they are to leave."

"No, my friend, it is good the man we are to take is parked like this and police they are gone. It will be best to have our camper facing the front of this car. You will be able to see our target. I will turn around. The traffic moves faster in that direction. You must get ready now. I am driving toward them now."

The camo man obeyed and opened the small rectangular window looking forward. He armed the RPG and took his position sighting on the middle of the windshield of Bonzac's car.

Chapter 32
The Main Objective

The explosion blew parts of Bonzac's car in all directions. The skull cap RPG man realized the mistake of having the rocket explode in front of them instead of with their vehicle behind. The driver's door was propelled through the right hand entrance of the school along with Bonzac's burning body. Most of the car's front end became fragmented and, including the engine, was sent to the right into on-coming traffic. The only vehicle that got hit and destroyed by the shrapneled car was the Winnebago.

The Winnebago's driver reacted with horror to their error as soon as the RPG rocket hit the car's windshield. "Cover your face, we are going to get hit with parts of the explosion."

For both the jihadists and their main objective, any attempt at finding safety was too late. The last visual experience by Bonzac and Flenk was a white flash. Their heads were immediately turned to a blenderized pulp which coated the flying pieces of disarticulated car. The two terrorists became victims of Bonzac's SUV engine as it smashed into the windshield of the Winnebago crushing both the driver and the RPG shooter. The driver saw it coming in the last two-seconds of life. It was enough time for him to shout, "We go to Paradise. Allah be praised."

Father Nesbitt was officiating in his capacity as Father confessor. He had one more hour to hear, exonerate, absolve, and dismiss the men and women who sought penance from the human errors they committed. His last confessor had a familiar voice.

"Father I have not visited the confessional for many years. I probably have committed many sins but mostly in the line of duty with my job. I can't really think of any specifics and I don't really have many regrets."

"Jesus was interested mainly in those actions and thoughts against others, which he deemed are correctable or have need of spiritual absolving through prayer." Nesbitt paused. "I somehow know your voice even though your confessions have not been presented to me before."

"Well, Father, I really needed to speak to you and this was the quickest way to do it. I'm Detective Bauman and I have serious information for you and the Dorfinkle woman."

"Ah, I knew it was a voice I've heard before. Should we go somewhere else to talk, Detective?" Nesbitt's could feel his pulse increase.

"No, what I have to say is that another incident occurred at the Drama School."

"What? Is Winnie okay?" *Please Lord let Winnie be spared.*

"Yes, she was inside. The explosion didn't penetrate beyond the front entrance. Most of the damage was outside. It involved mainly two vehicles. A parked SUV contained two victims identified by their drivers' licenses. They were Malcom Flenk and a known felon companion named Clement Bonzac. They were both killed by a rocket-propelled-grenade fired by an oncoming RV."

"Killed? Who fired the RPG?"

"There were two men in the RV without identification. One had an identifiable Islamic skull cap. The driver had the Winnebago's registration in his pants pocket. Both men died immediately from the SUV's engine sent into them from the explosion. Their attack didn't seem well-planned. They drove the RV right into the flying debris. Can you believe they were driving toward their target and couldn't figure out that this would happen?" Bauman took a deep breath. "We traced the registration to an RV leasing agency in Airmont, New York. Airmont is about thirty miles west of New York City. The man who leased the Winnebago is a green-card immigrant from Iraq. The home address he used turned out to be a septic tank pumping outfit. They had no Islamics employed there and never saw a Winnebago on their premises."

Nesbitt shuffled his seating position, "Wow, I never thought whoever was after me would eliminate their competition."

"That's about the only good news with this situation. However, it shows that whoever is after you will take out as many people as possible while going after their main objective—you."

"So Winnie is probably safe." Nesbitt emitted a sigh of relief.

"Not really, Father, these people will take out as many as they can. Ms. Dorfinkle could be collateral damage when she's with you or worse."

"What's worse, Detective?" Nesbitt leaned closer to the confessional window. His heart beat faster than ever.

"She could be kidnapped to get you out into the open or to a location of their choosing, which would be an area for a maximal kill zone."

Nesbitt began to sweat, "You mean like a church?"

"I mean like a church," Bauman replied.

Chapter 33
Aftershock

Winnie entered the classroom and sat in a front row seat. She was the center of attraction as she swirled around with a movie-star entrance. Only Professor Bangdot recognized her right away.

"I can tell immediately by your nun's headpiece Ms. Dorfinkle that you are not emulating a revival of The Flying Nun." Bangdot stood at the podium on the stage before the laughing class.

"I guess you all want me to explain. Well, how about my washer dryer are broken and the only thing in my wardrobe to wear today was my nun's habit."

More laughter, Bangdot smiled, "Try something else Winifred, my drama queen."

"Well, you know, even though I have a Jewish last name, I'm catholic. I could have been a nun. Except I never thought about it. I mean, I had a lot of boy friends growing up. Who thinks of being a nun, you know." Winnie turned to look at her smiling classmates.

A long-haired male student in the class stood up. "I saw you come into the building from an NYPD Police Car. What's the real story Winnie?"

Oh, dear, I can't really tell them. What should I say...? A sudden loud BOOM and the tinkle of breaking windows stopped further thought.

Bangdot ran to a window and shouted at his students, "Stay where you are. Whatever happened occurred on the street." He strained his head out the window letting in a blast of cold air with its definite cordite odor. He picked up the phone and talked to a security guard. Bangdot raised both palms. "No need to panic. Our guard tells me the police are already here. It looks like a bad car accident near our front entrance."

There could be no containing the incident at the Thespian Drama Academy address. Police radios were calling for backup at the Drama Academy. The words "possible terrorist detonated explosion" gave way to the arrival of two media helicopters running live TV breaking news interruptions on regular programming.

Winnie's pulse raced. She speed dialed Father Nesbitt. "Father, something happened again outside the Thespian's front entrance."

"I can see it from the TV coverage. Two vehicles are demolished and on fire. The Police are saying the fire in both cars has to be extinguished before they can even get close to the people inside either one."

"Is my police car coming for me? We're all okay inside the school, but I'm really scared."

"Winnie, just stay where you are. Yes, the same police will pick you up. Don't go with anyone else."

"Father, what do you mean?" Winnie's voice was tremulous.

"Just what I said. Don't go with any NYPD uniform other than those who took you to the Drama class."

"Father, do you think this was another attempt at me?"

"The news is calling it a motor vehicle collision between a parked car and a camper van. It may take a while for the fire and debris to be removed. Ambulances are being called for some pedestrians hit by fragments from the explosion. Just stay where you are with your Drama School people. Believe me it's safer than leaving at this point."

"My God, we just got a TV monitor. It looks awful. There can't be any survivors in those burning cars. How could it happen?"

"No one knows yet. Just wait. Call me every hour until you're on the way back with the police." Nesbitt looked at the TV news again. *This is no accident. It would take high speed by that camper to trigger such a disaster. The maximin speed on New York City streets with its slow traffic is never over thirty.*

"Every hour, okay Father." She disconnected and looked at the TV screen with the others. Most had their mouths open. Professor Bangdot stood again at the podium.

"Ahem…students, we are to resume our class while the incident outside is resolved. Perhaps Ms. Dorfinkle's guise as a nun has brought us safety from whatever happened out there."

Bangdot looked at Winnie.

She looked around the classroom and smiled, "Yes...yes...that's why I dressed up like a nun. It was to keep bad people away." She waited for the laughter to dissipate. "I mean, you know, nuns are like invisible people. I mean, when you seen a nun you immediately look another way. I know I always do."

Nesbitt met with his SEAL priests and addressed them around the television, "This is no simple vehicle collision. Right now we don't know if it's related to our situation. Two things are to be noted. First, this is the second violent episode in front of the Thespian Drama Academy. Winnie may have been the target again."

Ron, Del, and Hal stared at Nesbitt. Hal spoke first, "We have to find out who were in those vehicles."

"I'm afraid, we're going to have to sequester Winnie here at St. Patrick's." Nesbitt crossed his legs.

Del leaned forward at the edge of his folding chair, "Sir, we know what that means." Del looked at his two colleagues.

Nesbitt nodded in agreement, "You're all correct. By her staying in St. Patricks we're broadcasting to whoever is out there, that this is where we are. Come and get us."

Ron took a breath and let it out with slow words, "Guys, the next attack will be here at St. Patricks. It will most likely happen when the pews are full."

Nesbitt nodded in agreement again, "I'm going to alert the NYPD and State Police after I talk to Captain Craig at Navy Security."

"Zamir, Allah be praised, our van with our people is destroyed." Shahidi moved closer to the TV. "They must be in Paradise now."

Zamir sipped strong black coffee, "Yes, for what they have done. The other car contained the two who tried to assassinate the wrong priest and the girl. This leaves our mission to be at the St. Patrick's church. It is Allah's will that our people are sacrificed to help us succeed with our task."

Shahidi began pacing in the small room. "We must revisit our plan and look at all the options for access to the Nesbitt Priest. We do not care about the girl."

Chapter 34
St. Patrick's Cathedral

Detective Bauman met with Nesbitt again in Nesbitt's tiny St. Patrick's private dormitory-like room. "Father, this room is small to be your primary living space."

Nesbitt grinned, "I consider my living space, everywhere outside of this room. In here, I sit at my desk and sleep on my bed. Meals are in St. Pat's dining area. I've been where you work Detective. You're sitting one level above an open cubicle."

Bauman started to motion with his hand as Nesbitt raised his palm to interrupt his effort. "I know you have a life with a home, family, and domestic activities. I'm a Priest. My realm is this cathedral and my family is the clergy and the church with its multitude of spiritual devotees."

Bauman sat straight in the only chair next to Nesbitt's student-size desk. "All right, let's get to our current situation. My coming here was directed by the NYPD and the State Police. Neither of these organizations can commit to relocating their already short-staffed numbers to just wait for something to happen at St. Patricks." He swallowed from a bottle of water. "As soon as enemy suspects arrive or something happens in the cathedral, we'll mobilize all our available forces."

Nesbitt frowned, "It may be too late for that. Remember we're dealing with jihad terrorists. They want to kill me, yes, but their way of killing one person of interest is to also kill as many collateral infidels as possible. We really need people in place before the shit hits the fan. Pardon my profanity."

Bauman stood up. "Today, I'm just the messenger, Father. In this City, this is the best you're goin to get." He took a deep breath. "I have one more thing to report. It's both good and bad news."

"Okay, I'll take the good news first."

"Father, the news is both good and bad. We've confirmed identification of the victims in the car from the fiery accident yesterday. There was enough tissue obtainable to get a fingerprint from each of the two occupants—they were in fact Flenk and Bonzac."

"So this was a second try at Winnie." Nesbitt remained seated and held eye contact with Bauman.

Bauman leaned closer to Nesbitt, "And the Al Qaeda were after them. We were able to trace the camper van to two green card Islamics from an address in a rundown two-bedroom house near a chemical plant in Newark, New Jersey. The two were stupid enough to give the camper rental company their real IDs and home location in order to get the rental."

Nesbitt was open-mouthed and slowly let out his thoughts, "The Al Qaeda wanted to eliminate Flenk so they could use all their resources and get credit for getting me."

"The State Police have contacted the Feds about this. Unfortunately, they also have to wait for something to happen before they commit any of their units." Bauman finished his water. "I'll not ask what you have in mind, but call me if anything or anyone is suspect."

Nesbitt went to the nun's quarters. Most of the occupants were in the main church in a small chapel in noontime prayer. An elder nun sat at a narrow desk.

"Can I help you Father?" Her smile resulted in a roadmap of elderly wrinkles.

"I'm looking for Winifred Dorfinkle." He fingered his large cross and chain.

"Who?" The senior woman looked at her roster of nuns who had checked out and those still in their spartan rooms. "I see no such person in our ranks, Father."

"Ms. Dorfinkle is not actually one of our nuns, Sister. She's here seeking sanctuary while a dangerous situation outside is being resolved."

"Oh dear, I'll not ask the details. Let me look in our charity log. We usually have a few displaced persons from home fires or from domestic violence placement." She seemed flustered at not being successful.

Nesbitt leaned closer and spoke softer, "She'll be the one the police picked up yesterday and brought back last evening."

A smile brought more lines to the cracked facial skin, "Oh yes, here it is. The NYPD signed for her both times. I'll ring her room and have her come into the small lobby."

"Can't I see her in her room?"

"Please father, no strangers, especially men, are allowed beyond this desk. Even the police wait in the lobby."

His response was almost robotic, "I certainly understand and applaud your adherence to our Lord's dictates for appropriate security for safety and sanctity."

Nesbitt walked the few steps to the maroon-carpeted lobby. The only furniture was a black two-cushion sofa with matching parlor chairs facing it over a round glass-top coffee table. A New Testament Bible was the only adornment on the table. The area had a musty odor and the sunlight beaming through the only window made abundant dust particles move about in random search for a place to settle. Winnie came in adjusting her nun's white crucifix and chain.

She sat on a chair facing Nesbitt on the sofa. Her movement on the chair caused a dust turmoil amidst a weary beam of light. "I'm so glad to see you, Father. Have you any news about the incident yesterday at the School?"

"Yes, I have." Nesbitt told her of the identity of the two vehicle dead and the implications.

"Why so solemn? It means there are no more people trying to kill me."

He maintained his somber face, "I'm afraid it means that the next attack is by the Islamic Arabs after me. They'll try to get me and as many others along with us to best effect a widely publicized terrorist action."

She raised here eyebrows, "But I'm isolated here in the nun's quarters."

He patted his left hand next to him on the sofa, "Sit here. I want to keep my voice down."

Winnie smiled and immediately moved across to sit at his side. She adjusted her flowing black habit and moved next to him pressing herself against his left hip.

"Why are you sitting so close, Winnie? Don't forget the rules of propriety for the Nuns' Quarters."

She smiled and touched his left hand. "I don't want you to forget that I'm no nun. You kissed me, remember?"

He ignored the remark, "Winnie, we think the attempt will come at the last Mass service between five and six o'clock."

"What are you and the other fake priests going to do?"

"We want everything to seem normal at the Mass. As soon as we see someone or some small group out of place, we'll send a signal to the NYPD and others waiting for our call."

Winnie frowned, "But you don't even know who to look for. I mean, what does this guy from Iraq looks like now?"

"That's true, however, our 'fake' priests have spotted some Middle-Eastern types tracking Dr. Potts and Professor Bangdot. They've taken pictures with their cell phone cameras." He squeezed her hand. "And you're correct about Shahidi, the Iraqi. It would really help if we knew his appearance today. He was injured like me and may have had surgery that's altered his appearance."

She responded to the pressure of his hand, "Oh Forbish dear, I can't just vegetate in my virginal room here," She rapidly put her right hand to her mouth. "Oh, and I have to tell you, I'm not a virgin. I mean I had a few first times in high school and some casual things when I first came to New York. Oh, Father Nesbitt, I have to be a part of this."

Nesbitt turned his face to her, "We could use someone to help with the monitoring who could move fast in the sanctuary to warn us. Someone who would not be noticed."

Her eyes widened and she smiled, "You mean like a nun. Like me?" She threw her arms around his neck and kissed him.

The kiss lingered. Winnie moved a few inches apart and Nesbitt said, "Yes, like you." *Dear God please watch over her.*

Chapter 35
Books for St. Patricks

Zamir finished packing a box of books. "We got these just in time for this evening's attack on St. Patricks."

Shahidi picked up one of the hymn books. They were all black with a silver crucifix and silver printing on the covers. He opened a book and touched a small brick of Semtex placed in the square cutout of the page sections. "This is a lot of explosive. How are we all going to survive?"

"Omar, it is about timing. Let us look again at our schedule and the St. Patrick agenda for the day." Zamir flattened out the folded St. Patrick's flyer he had picked up during a church tour. "It has each day's schedule for this week. A memorial service will be after the hours of lunch. I will have these books brought in to replace some old volumes." He moved his finger lower on the list of the day's events. "See here the name of the priest for the small closet—it is called the confessional. LCDR Nesbitt will be there from four-to-six o'clock listening to the infidels beg their God for forgiveness."

"Zamir, remember, it is I who must personally destroy the Navy man who is now a Priest."

"Yes, yes, yes, it will be you. You will go into his booth. Here, I have the words you must say to him. You must practice. You will succeed, Omar. You have no accent with your English."

Shahidi nodded, "And once he is dead, I will leave and give a signal outside for the sidewalk vendor to trigger the books to end the existence of those infidels denying our Allah."

"It will be so, Omar. Now, say those words to me like you are to speak to the Navy Priest."

Shahidi looked at the sheet and put it down. He looked directly at Zamir and spoke, "Forgive me Father, for I have sinned. It has been many years since my last confession."

Two SEALs coded as S1 and S2 sent from Captain Craig's Navy Security detail finished setting up the TV monitors and cameras. The cameras were aimed at the front entrance to the sanctuary, the pews closest to the confessional booths, and the center altar set up for the late afternoon Mass. A SEAL Lieutenant JG adjusted the focus and had three stools placed in the tiny monitor room that was once functional as the janitorial supply closet.

S1 looked at Winnie in her Nun's outfit. "Sister, you are to look at the screen showing the aisle next to the confessional. If you see anyone who violates any Catholic mannerism, give us the alert. We have cell phones and a fax machine for external communications and warnings."

"Okay, I don't know whether I'm excited or just nervous. I'm an expert on confessionals. I confess to stuff, you know, a lot." Winnie crossed herself and kissed her crucifix.

S1 smiled, "Okay, but it's extremely important that if you see even the slightest gesture which is not according to what pious Catholics do is wrong or out of place, you must tell us."

"I will. You can count on me. And thanks for picking out this closet." Winnie's face blushed, reddening her nose.

"Why is this closet so important?" S2 asked her.

"I mean, you know, the bathroom is right next to us. Ever since I woke up I've had the urge to pee every two hours. You don't know what a chore that is to do wearing this nun's outfit."

S2 smiled with his response, "Sister, I hope I never have to personally find out."

Winnie crossed herself, "I'm not really a nun, you know. I don't think I'll ever get the calling to be one either, you know. I mean, nun's don't have dreams about bananas like I do."

S1 stared at her with a wrinkled brow, "Whatever you are, Sister, just focus on the monitor screen."

Another person was doing exactly what the team inside the monitor room was doing—using his unassisted God-given vision. He eyed each person as they entered. He emptied the janitor implements for the Navy SEALs. He was scrutinizing all attendees throughout the afternoon.

One thing and one thing only was bothering him. It was gnawing at his inherent suspicion of all things normal to St. Patricks. What occurred was only somewhat questionable. It happened right after the first afternoon memorial service.

One of the Deacon's assistants was responsible for the maintenance of the literature, offering packets, and supplying agenda sheets. Placement of the packets and agendas were done early in the morning. Every calendar quarter, the condition of the hymn books was inspected and replacements, repairs, and new Vatican-Approved works were appropriately placed. Today, some hymn books were the target. The one's ailing were collected and replaced. This was not announced at the morning reading of the day's agenda. In fact, the two men who performed the activity were unknown to him. He felt like a great burden was resting on his shoulders. The only way to unload it was to inform the three people in the monitor room. He had to act. He went up the left aisle toward the janitor room.

The hairs on Winnie's neck beneath her flowing head piece started to tingle. She looked at the screen. Something was out of place. She recognized the man immediately. Winnie pointed to the screen for the left aisle and alerted her two SEALS.

"My God, it's Montague Kelp. He's coming this way. He's moving fast."

Chapter 36
The Face from Arizona

Over a thousand miles away, Adem Saleem had been having a sensation of a lump in his throat. At times it became difficult to swallow. Today it was the worst it had been for the past two weeks. His wife insisted he see his doctor. Saleem was frustrated at first. He finally made his decision when his wife pointed out an important fact to him.

Mrs. Saleem faced him after his morning prayers. "Adem, you have your feelings in your throat and in your mind only after you do your Salat. Allah, is giving you these sensations. You must act on this. See a doctor, tell him the story. You must call a government agency. See Dr. Alibahn. He is a throat specialist. He is of our faith."

ENT physician Mendi Alibahn adjusted his head mirror and placed a dry wooden tongue blade in Saleem's mouth. "Say ahhhhh, please." He probed deeper. "Say again…the ahhhhh."

Saleem complied.

The doctor relaxed and looked at Saleem's vital signs. The temperature and blood pressure were normal. However, his pulse was definitely elevated. "Mr. Saleem, I see nothing physically wrong in your throat. Your x-rays show only mild sinus thickening. However, you are breathing at a very fast rate. Your lungs are clear. Your oxygen saturation is normal."

"But, doctor, I know something it is wrong."

"There is one thing that is not normal, Mr. Saleem. You are breathing through your mouth. This causes the dryness and sensation of difficulty to swallow. You humidify your throat and sinuses by allowing air to pass through your nose. You must breath through your nose and drink additional water." Dr. Alibahn sat back and removed his head mirror. "Something is bothering you. You are breathing too fast and your heart is beating faster than normal. This is a sign that you are very nervous—that you are thinking about something of great concern in your life. Your wife has told our nurse that it might be about a time you went on vacation. Perhaps you can tell me of this."

For the first time in weeks, Saleem felt relief. Initially, he was angry that his wife kept urging him to call someone in the US Government. Her words replayed in his head: "But I do not want to draw attention to us. We have good records as American citizens."

Mrs. Saleem tugged at his sleeve, "Saleem, all you have to do is call someone who is important to immigration." She was unrelenting. "You must first see a doctor about your throat. Tell the doctor about what happened in New York City with the one you feel is on a jihad."

The Doctor listened and accessed his consultation communication folder on his computer. "I tend to agree with your wife. I'll print out a number for you to call. You may use me as a reference. You will not get into trouble. If you feel something bad about this man then you must speak up. It is affecting your health. I will be telling this to the people you call."

Saleem dialed the first phone number Dr. Alibahn had written for him. A woman's voice answered, "Federal Bureau of Investigation, how can I help you."

He looked at his wife, "It is a woman. How can a woman be of help?"

Mrs. Saleem glared at her husband, "Adem, this is America. Women have the rights of the men. If you do not speak up, I will do it."

Saleem spoke, "It is Adem Saleem speaking. I must report that an arrival from Iraq is perhaps on a Jihad."

"Iraq? Jihad? That's Middle East Section, just a moment I'll connect you."

A few seconds of rapid clicks was followed by a male voice, "Middle East Office, Agent Peter Pudder speaking."

Saleem swallowed some water, "I am American Citizen, Adem Saleem. My wife and I wish to report one who is perhaps on a Jihad. He is from New York City."

Saleem described their Empire State Building events and described the man and his words. He looked at the business card Shahidi had given him and read from it.

Pudder was used to such calls. Most were false alarms. He clicked on a special icon. "Just a minute, I'll use our computer to scan for any alerts for New York City. And thank you for being open to possible anti-American behavior. You are a good citizen." Pudder looked at his screen's readout. The listing were this year's items, which were called in and acted upon by the Agency.

Saleem rolled his amber worry beads in his left hand, "Is there any thing else I can do. I have picture of the man from our New York trip."

"Over a hundred entries of complaints and suspicious behaviors had been reported so far this year for New York City." Pudder tried to narrow his listing. "Mr. Saleem did you see this man at any other tourist sites?"

"We went to visit many places in New York City. Wait…my wife she speaks to me." Saleem listened to her. "She reminds me of only one other place we did see this man from Iraq. It was a tour of the Christian Church place called St. Patrick's Cathedral."

Pudder added St. Patrick's to his data input. "Very good, Mr. Saleem, can you please email me the photos you have with this man? I'll give you the email address."

Chapter 37
The Bureaucracy Web

FBI Special Agent Peter Pudder waited for the computer screen to digest the added information. Suddenly over twelve lines began blinking a fluorescent green. The St. Patrick's links were rated high priority.

"Mr. Saleem, I have to ask you and your wife to come to our office. It is extremely important. You are not in any trouble. Please bring all of your pictures that have the man in them. Please give me your address and we'll send a car for you."

Saleem's mouth got dryer, "Is it for good purpose? Did I do correct as a citizen of the United States?"

"Yes, indeed, Mr. Saleem, I wish we had more people as vigilant as you. I'll talk to you later when we meet."

Pudder studied the superscripts at the end of each flagged entry on his computer screen. He spoke aloud to his administrative assistant, "Gretchen, I need a top secret printout of my screen. Also dispatch a car to this address to bring these two people to the Chief's reception room. I have phone calls to make on my separate lines."

The red-haired admin smiled, "Great, I was just thinking about how slow things were around here. What's up?"

"I don't know yet, but after I talk to the Chief, we have to do a merge conference line with the CIA, Immigration, and…you're not going to believe this…the Department of the Navy."

Gretchen made the call for the car to Saleem's home while staring at her boss. "Navy, Peter?"

"Yes, a Navy Special Security division within the SEALs." He grabbed the material from the printer after emailing everything from Saleem's discourse to his boss. He gave Gretchen one more look, "Something big is going down in New York City."

The CIA was contacted by the Chief FBI Agent in Arizona. "Yes, that's right. I got hits from your group, immigration, and the Navy. Let me give you the trigger items."

The CIA Director in Arizona was wide-eyed at the alert signal he got from the St. Patrick's input. "Wow, this could be huge."

CIA Headquarters in Langley, Virginia received the information from their Arizona office. The alert was sent directly to the Middle East Affairs Division, Office of US Terrorism. CIA Senior Agent Manning Poore looked at his computer screen while talking on a conference phone to the Arizona sender. Poore was in a "situation room" with five other agents. He read the transmittals to his team. All were dressed in dark navy blue suits and maroon neckties.

Poore summarized the importance of the message, "What I have from our Director is the following. First, CIA is to be involved in any action in New York City centered around St. Patrick's Cathedral and...this I don't understand...the Thespian Drama Academy...also located in New York City. Our orders are to alert all CIA Agents in those locales after receipt of suspicious activity. So far we have nothing threatening going on with St. Patrick's. However this Drama School is another story."

The three men and two women around the conference table remained silent and anticipatory for further data. Poore continued, "We are not to engage in any hands-on action until specific terrorism attacks occur. What we are to do is to focus observation units around all known Islamic activist cells in a fifty mile radius around and in New York City itself."

An excited female raised her hand, "Sir, what are we looking for?"

"We've activated the satellite cameras covering this area. Any activity from any of these cells, such as people moving from their addresses and heading into New York City, is cause for surveillance and readiness for extreme sanction."

A burly agent raised his hand, "Is this a pure CIA assignment, sir?"

"The FBI got first alert. They already have their agents walking the streets and cruising in cars around both sites. Also, I have a report from NYPD and the FBI of a

terrorist RPG action agains a vehicle parked outside a drama school."

The Agent continued his thought, "Why didn't the
NYPD activate Federal action, sir."

Poore sat back, "The usual reason is one of turf. The
original flag on these two sites in the City gives the NYPD
priority."

The female Agent frowned, "I hope those fuckers in
the FBI don't grab action for grandstand PR."

Poore grinned, "No, and please do not use profane
adjectives when talking about our Federal relatives." After
the laughter waned he added, "The priority team has already infiltrated both sites. The ball-carrier for this action is
the Navy SEALs."

Poore read more on the history of the situation including the identity of Father Nesbitt as the target of an
Iraqi Jihadist from a previous military action. "In short, the
Navy flushes the enemy out and we contain and round them
up for isolation and prosecution." Poore paused and held up
a recent fax photo. "We do have a picture of what the prin-
cipal attacker looks like." He cleared his throat. "Compli-
ments of the Arizona FBI."

The CIA Agents around the table stared with one
questioning word—"Arizona"?

Father Nesbitt's diligence was ahead of Adem
Saleem, the FBI, and CIA. He contacted Captain Craig

immediately after the Drama School RPG incident. "Yes sir, their next action has to be St. Patricks."

Captain Craig was with his executive officer and two senior SEAL Officers. "Okay Forbish, give us the worst projection."

Nesbitt was with his three pseudo-priests, "Shahidi will have to come to us, here. He'll try to isolate me and then institute an action against as many church goers in attendance as possible. We have to assume it will be tomorrow."

Craig tapped his pen on a pad near the phone, "Forbish, I'm sending two surveillance experts to set up monitors. We'll also have more SEALs attending Mass and other activities in civilian clothes. However, I can't deploy the combat unit until a threat is recognized as imminent. Remember, the military is not supposed to be engaged in any domestic violence unless ordered by the President."

Nesbitt wrinkled his brow, "What about the locals and the other Feds?"

"They're also on standby alert. Believe me, this is the best way. If the FBI or CIA are appointed in charge here, they'll fight each other for priority and could screw up the whole operation. We do have an alert from the CIA. They have contact with someone who has a photo of a person-of-interest, taken during a tour of the Empire State Building. We'll send it as soon as we get it."

"Okay, sir, we're exerting due diligence as we speak. And thank you for the ordnance and protective vests for our real priests and St. Patrick staff."

Craig chuckled, "No problem, how did it go over with the Monsignor?"

"The clergy is like the military, sir. If this turns into a disaster, he'll end up doing missionary work in Greenland for the rest of his life. If it succeeds, he gets awards and a promotion." Nesbitt paused, "He's willing to take a risk and his enthusiasm is infectious. His entire staff see this as a calling of the highest order."

Craig sighed, "I just hope they don't meet Jesus sooner than they expected. Do you believe in the power of prayer, Forbish?"

"Sometimes, sir, and this is one of those times."

"I'm flying in to New York City tonight. I'll contact you later." Craig rubbed his chin in thought and looked at his colleague SEALs. "The same goes for us too, gentlemen. If we win, we get medals, and maybe promotions. If we lose, we get permanent assignments in Alaska's outermost Aleutian Islands forever."

Chapter 38
The Confessional

"Zamir, the weather it is very cold. It will slow us down when we leave the St. Patrick's front entrance." Shahidi put on a below-the-knee length dark grey coat.

Zamir responded with a laugh, "But it is good for us to gain entrance. The church may not be using metal detectors. Such may be against the high church as dictated by the Vatican. Such a security presence they interpret as keeping worshippers away. It is not so with our mosques." He opened Shahidi's coat before he buttoned it. "And you see that there is good concealment in the coat for weapons."

"But I will not have a weapon until I get to the booth of confession, remember?"

Zamir smiled again, "Yes, I taped it under the chair for you inside the small place of confession. And all the explosives are the plastique which cannot be detected as metal."

Shahidi put on a black scarf, "I think we are ready. Are our outside people in place? It is noon time now. We must leave to get into the church for when the Navy Nesbitt enters the confession booth."

"It will only take us one hour. We will be early. And our people in front of the church across the street are there now selling infidel food."

"What is infidel food?" Shahidi walked to the front door.

"The unholy sausage called by them as 'hot dogs'. They also have hot coffee drinks. It is a good cover for a very cold day. The hot dog people will give the signal to the ones waiting in parked cars to detonate the books. It will be once we pass the food stalls with the large umbrellas and you give them the signal."

Shahidi left the Suffern house with Zamir and entered their car. Once inside, Shahidi ventilated another of his fears, "I am not happy with us leaving the church explosions by the underground trains, Zamir."

"It is perfect, Omar. The trains are usually crowded. And New York people are strange in crowds. They do not look at each other. They will never be able to identify us ."

Zamir walked beside Shahidi. "It is important that we go to the first gatherings inside the church. We do not have to leave. People will be coming and going even when a service is underway. I will begin the exchange of the song books when people they arrive for the early service. There will only be one hour until you are to go to the confession place. You will be the fourth person for Father Nesbitt. The church has already gathered a list from the people who worship. I entered your name yesterday after I hid the pistol for you."

They waited until the flow of people became steady. Most attendees were by twos. No one seemed to be scrutinizing them as they passed through the center bronze door. Zamir began collecting the worn hymn books as another accomplice attendee appeared with the new hymn book replacements. The boxes for the old and the new books had arrived with the regular delivery of supplies for St. Patrick's day-to-day operation.

&

The memorial service drew a lot of people. Twenty rows of pews were reserved for the mourners and friends of the deceased. The side row nearest the confessionals was at the twenty-eight row marker, which was already occupied by the Mass attendees. Shahidi positioned himself at the aisle seat three pews down from the booth. He felt slightly relaxed after he saw that the other civilian occupants were dressed as he was. *I am truly blending in. Allah favors me for success in my holy mission.*

&

Nesbitt received his first confessor exactly at 4-o'clock. It was an elderly lady with a tremulous voice clutching rosary beads. He gave out an audible sigh as he removed his right hand from a double-edged boot knife. He did, however, keep his cell phone at the ready to press the button which would summon his team to confront the enemy. Nesbitt listened to the woman.

"Father forgive me, for I have sinned. My husband has recently died and I have not yet informed Social Security or his pension office."

"Why do you consider this a sin?" Nesbitt looked at the small red light on his phone. If it blinks it means terrorists have been sighted in the sanctuary.

"I've received checks in his name. We're retired and I need the full amount of our retirement income to survive in New York City. When I report his death, I collect only his Social Security and only half his pension."

Nesbitt listened to her. *I must still do my job to our faithful constituents.* "You could face financial problematic fines if you do not. Cheating is a sin as is any type of theft. You must report the information. Most organizations are behind in bringing up-to-date such changes. I also understand there are extensions and forgiveness allowances to the newly bereaved."

The woman coughed, "And what of the church, Father?"

"Performing the right actions will be the correct pathway to salvation. As you contact the proper agencies do so holding your rosary. All will be well. You also should consider a change to a more affordable address. Do you have family in the City?"

"Yes, Father, they have invited me but I don't want to be a burden."

"Go to them and the imagined burden you bring here today will be lifted." Nesbitt looked at his watch as the woman left.

A college student appeared after Nesbitt heard a lawyer's confession of infidelity. The student's perceived sins revolved around engaging in a fraternity prank which resulted in a physical injury to a pledge.

Nesbitt looked at his watch. It was already 5-o'clock. He removed his 9 mm automatic from his inside pocket. *Something has to happen soon.*

The student responded to Nesbitt's silence. "Father, are you still there? How should I right this wrong?"

"We are all responsible for the outcome of our actions, my son. If you were part of the planning as well as part of the execution of the episode, then you must bear the penalties of the consequence. You must atone to God with ten 'Our Fathers' and ten 'Hail Mary's.'"

I feel so isolated. I'll be unable to help the others outside the confessional. He glanced at the card for his scheduled confessions. *One more to go. It has to be this next one.* A scary thought popped into his head. *What if it is not to be a person-to-person confrontation? What if the confessional is wired with explosives?*

He pressed the button for the outside light to turn from red to green. The last person on the list entered. Nesbitt looked again at the list. No names or initials were allowed. Each attendee's identity was held in confidentiality. With time a priest gets to know his frequent confessor. Winnie was an easy example. He got to recognize her voice and flighty discourse after their first session.

Nesbitt braced himself as a large man settled between him and the black mesh screen. The man cleared his throat and spoke in a clear friendly voice, "Forgive me Father Nesbitt, for I have sinned. It has been several years since my last confession."

Nesbitt pressed the red button.

Chapter 39
Infidels

"Who is that you say?" The lead SEAL stretched his neck to look at Winnie's TV monitor.

"Montague Kelp, he's a sort of janitor and guard for St. Patrick's. He's helping Father Nesbitt's Navy team." Winnie held her line of sight at the monitor. "He's heading for our closet. Something must be happening."

Kelp knocked on the door and entered as soon as it was unlocked. He looked from Winnie to the two SEALS. Kelp was used to Winnie dressed as a nun. It was the first time he saw any of the new Navy men. The two SEALs were in black BDUs. Their attached weapons, communication microphones, protective vests, and pistol ammo magazine pouches gave their normal muscular appearance one of football-player bulk.

Winnie quickly introduced him, "This is Montague Kelp. What's up Monty? I mean, you know, why did you move fast up the aisle?"

The JG SEAL stared at Kelp. He took in Kelp's formidable and ugly appearance and thought he could be what Quasimodo of the Hunchback of Notre Dame might look like without the hunchback.

Kelp slowed his breathing and pointed to the monitors. "One man is here who should not be here. Scroll back ten minutes on your screen Ms. Dorfinkle."

The JG stared at Winnie, "Dorfinkle, and you're a nun?"

Winnie manipulated her keyboard until Kelp gave her a command.

"Stop, there, the two men changing the hymn books. They are not the staff who usually do this. I don't know them. We must look at the books." Kelp's sense of urgency raised the groups adrenalin levels.

The second SEAL spoke, "We have to isolate and immobilize those two before we touch the books. They may have phones or detonating devices on their person."

The JG pressed his red button, "This is S1 and S2 on monitor. Two suspects may have planted ordnance in hymn books. LCDR Nesbitt what are your orders?"

There was no response from Nesbitt.

"I repeat sir, unless you reply now, I will assume an action response."

Still no answer.

S1 sprang to command, "S3, S4, S5 remove all hymn books that may contain explosive to the outside of the Cathedral once we have the terrorists neutralized. Mr. Kelp will assist." S3, S4, and S5 were codes for Nesbitt's three pseudo-priests: Ron, Del, and Hal.

S1 turned to Winnie, "Okay, Sister Garfunkle, you're promoted to keep your eyes on these monitor screens. If you see anything else, press the red button on the phone we gave you. Just press it and talk. Give us your message. It will be transmitted to all our phones."

Winnie's eyes widened, her pulse raced, and her face reddened, "First, my name is Dorfinkle and I am not a nun. You don't have to call me Sister anything. Second, what am I to do if I'm the only one free to move about?"

"One of us will give you instruction," S1 responded.

Winnie felt sweat under her arms in the warm nun frock, "What about Father Nesbitt? What's happened to him? Why doesn't he say anything? Oh my God, maybe he's in trouble."

S1 looked at the monitors. He ignored Winnie's query. S3, S4, and S5 were walking the aisle waiting for their cue to remove the deadly hymn books. "We have to go now. I see where our two targets are." He turned to S2, "You take the one at the right entrance door. I'll take the other in the middle. We have to get them at the same time. They must not utter a sound or fall down. You know what to do."

⤙

Nesbitt didn't know what responders would be coming his way. He had to act fast. He knew his last confessional was Omar Shahidi. Shahidi had made a mistake. *Should I use the gun or the knife?*

⤙

Shahidi removed the taped-.380 Beretta automatic from under the wooden compartment separator as soon as he sat down. He moved the gun's slide back to make sure it was loaded for firing and gave his prelude to confession. "Forgive me Father Nesbitt, for I have sinned. It has been several years since my last confession."

Nesbitt's immediate alert first came because of Shahidi's gun. Zamir had already loaded it. A cartridge was already in the chamber. When Shahidi ratcheted the chamber, that round automatically ejected and bounced around the tiny plywood cabin. Secondly, Shahidi did not say Father, forgive me, he said Forgive me Father Nesbitt. The name of the confessional priest was not to be uttered and the first word is Father not Forgive me father.

Nesbitt didn't want gunfire which could start a panic or might activate a preemptive attack on the worshippers at the Mass. He immediately extended his left arm in a lightening Karate move, which went straight through the thin mesh wooden separator. His fist struck Shahidi's right hand knocking the .380 pistol to the floor of the dark booth.

Shahidi reacted with a reflex kick to the disintegrated separator just as Nesbitt threw his body toward his surprised adversary. The resultant violent movement of the two combatants caused the booth to move from side-to-side. Shahidi pressed the speed dial on his phone. Zamir did not respond.

Several worshipers were listening to the Priest announcing the eucharist. The only person who seemed to be interested in the rocking confessional booth was Winnie.

"Oh my God! Something's happening in Father Nesbitt's confessional!" Winnie made the announcement as soon as she saw it. No one else was with her in the janitor closet. She looked to the church entry doors. S1 and S2 were in the process of immobilizing the two terrorists. Suddenly some words came from S1.

"S3.. S4, S5 and Montague Kelp collect all hymn books. Have the congregation pass them to the end of each pew and get them outside quick. We'll meet you out there to help Kelp inactivate any planted explosives. Don't let anyone leave yet. If the congregation starts to leave in panic, a terrorist out front might signal detonation."

Winnie yelled into her phone again. "I think Father Nesbitt needs help." There was no answer.

"Oh my God!" Winnie saw the booth was starting to fall apart with the vigorous motion. She dashed out of the janitor closet and ran to the confessional. Her flowing nun habit was moving like a flapping black flag with her black and white headpiece raised in the air like a cape for her head. She could hear two voices conversing in a foreign language.

Nesbitt grunted his words in Farsi while locked in arm grips with Shahidi, "Omar, I know you're doing this out of revenge."

"Priest or Navy man, you have killed my family. Allah has willed that I trained to punish you and other non-believers." Shahidi maneuvered his right knee to press on

Nesbitt's chest. He exerted all his strength and separated their connection sending Nesbitt and the confessional's door flying into the aisle. The momentum of the movement brought Shahidi to the floor at Winnie's feet.

Winnie looked down at Nesbitt covered by the full-length confessional-booth door. She switched her gaze to Shahidi who was stretching his hands toward his fallen Beretta.

✢

S3, S4, and S5 were collecting explosive-packed hymn books into a large box held by Kelp. Once the box was full, Kelp handed an empty box to S5 and ran to the right side exit church door to place the container at the farthest spot from the cathedral. He ran back for another packed crate.

S1 spoke into his hand-held walkie-talkie. "All priests for the Mass please direct all worshipers out the left side entrances immediately."

✢

Shahidi heard the order from Nesbitt's device. "I want to see your face." He pushed the confessional door from atop Nesbitt. "It is you. You are the killer of my brother and parents. Allah has willed me to take your life and the life of your infidel followers at prayer to a false God." Shahidi stretched his right leg to reach the .380. Suddenly he felt great pain between his legs and shrieked in agony.

Winnie the nun, grabbed Shahidi's scrotum with both hands and squeezed his testicles as hard as she could.

Nesbitt rolled to his left side and stood up grabbing the rail of an aisle pew. He couldn't believe his eyes as he focused on Winnie's hands in a vice-like grip on Shahidi's genitals. His walkie-talkie gave him a capsule of the action around him.

Kelp's raspy voice came on, "Okay that's the last of them. They're outside in the tight nest of oak trees. I pulled all the wires from the plastique, so go find Father Nesbitt."

S1 spoke loud on his device, "Roger that, we've got the two terrorists inside who changed the hymn books. Father Nesbitt, do you read me. Over."

Nesbitt touched Winnie's shoulder, "Winnie, let go. I'll handle him now."

Winnie turned her red face toward Nesbitt. It gave Shahidi a chance to push her away and head for the left exit with the rest of the fleeing congregation.

Shahidi dashed outside still agonizing over the dull ache in his groin. He felt like throwing up, but knew he had to find the hot dog stand to give the signal to trigger the explosives. *It is my only chance now to destroy the group of non-believers and the Navy priest with them.*

Chapter 40
Rush Hour

Shahidi pushed through the crowd moving from the left cathedral doors toward the outside. He could see the red-and-yellow umbrella of the hot dog cart. He waved his arms in the air but could not get the man's attention.

The hot dog man's orders were to press the red-lit button on his device when Shahidi gave him the order. Five-Minutes after the red button activation he was to press the green-lit button to trigger the blast. He looked around at the disorder of men and women heading toward him.

Shahidi shouldered his way toward the cart-man and reached him severely short of breath. He couldn't phonate any words. He grabbed the man's right arm and finally let out the order. "It is I, messenger from Allah. Send the infidels from this life."

The hot dog man extended a silvery antenna. Five minutes later the hot dog man pressed the green button. He threw himself under his cart expecting a violent explosion.

Shahidi ran across the wide street between honking cars and taxis. He went as fast as he could down the entrance to the subway station. Shahidi looked back as he approached the turnstile, which let his day-pass grant him passage. There were no screams or dust clouds or sirens. There were only two figures that stood out like back-lit effigies. One was in a full length black robe and narrow white rectangular neck piece as part of the collar. The other was the woman dressed in black with a trailing white head-covering.

ᔐ

Nesbitt wanted Shahidi alive if possible. He knew Shahidi wanted him dead. Nesbitt's line of sight was fixed on Shahidi's slow forceful-pushing through the commuter crowd. He was unaware that Winnie was right behind him as he leaped over the station turnstile lifting up a length of his dress-like black vestment. He vaguely heard some off-color remark behind him.

Winnie lifted her black flowing nun outfit to emulate Nesbitt, but got caught in one of the turnstile's rounded blunt blades. Part of her garment tore. The baggy culotte black pants, however, remained caught as she tried to shorten the distance between her and Father Nesbitt. She let out a curse as she felt cold air now attacking her behind and legs, "Fuckshitassbitchcock."

ᔐ

Shahidi pushed his way to the entrance of a Downtown subway car. The interior was packed with commuters and he became wedged among a group of predominantly female workers. Shahidi puffed his exhalations and grabbed for a vertical pole for support. His groin was still throbbing. He looked around. A few other passengers were also breathing heavily from dashing and pushing into the subway car. He twisted to see out the still open door to find Nesbitt getting closer. The woman in the nun clothes was also in pursuit. Many of the crowd behind Winnie were staring at her back. Some were pointing and most were laughing at the bare area exposed when her habit was partially torn off.

⸎

The subway car door was blocked as the car filled to capacity. Nesbitt rapidly changed his direction to the car ahead, which seemed to have some free space. Winnie followed him into the car just as the doors moved shut. Nesbitt was five passengers from Winnie. He raised his hand and waved her forward to his side.

Winnie decided to take advantage of her nun status. "Please people, I must talk to the Priest over there." The pressure of the packed riders lessened as she wriggled between several men and reached Nesbitt.

"Winnie, the man I'm after is in that car," He pointed to Shahidi's car adjacent to theirs. "Look, I don't want you to follow me in there. He may have a gun or knife or something."

Winnie grabbed his arm, "No, Father, you look. I helped you out back at the confessional. I'm doing my damndest to keep you alive. Ooop!" She jumped closer into his arms.

"What's with the hug? This is no time for socialization."

"Father, I wasn't socializing. I mean, you know, I don't mind getting intimate with you anytime, but someone just grabbed a handful of my ass. Some protection from gropers these nun habits are."

Nesbitt glared at the man behind her. The passenger squeezed away from them. Nesbit spoke to Winnie's ear, "How could you feel anything through those black robes?" He looked over her shoulder to her rear and could not contain smiling. "Winnie, I think your black gown has shed some of its cloth."

Winnie couldn't turn or move her arms to explore the area in question. "What are you talking about? We have to get to that badass in the other car."

Nesbitt didn't want to have any witness to his feeling Winnie's rear anatomy so he whispered in her ear. "Winnie, everyone behind you is admiring your red polka-dot bikini panties."

"How did you know...?" She finally got an arm around to touch her behind and reddened. "How did that happ....oh dear...the turnstile. I remember getting stuck, but I didn't feel or hear anything tear."

Nesbitt felt the train reach its peak acceleration. "All right, I'll walk behind you and literally cover your derriere. We've got to get into Shahidi's car fast."

Chapter 41
Subway to Paradise

The subway train began its deceleration into the next stop. Passengers wanting to leave started to push and elbow for position as close to the doors as possible. This action created moveable space near the doors connecting them to Shahidi's car.

Nesbitt grabbed Winnie's shoulders and moved her toward the car's connecting doors. He spoke to her ear again. "I'm sure he's seen us and especially you with your white carapace and black outfit. Discard your head piece now. He'll be looking for a nun and me along with her. I'll let you steer. Head straight for the connector door. I'll have my head between your shoulder blades."

Winnie's visual picture was different, "Promise not to stare down at my undies."

"Oh for God's sakes, Winnie, we're in a life-and-death situation here. Wait until someone pushes the connecting door open and follow-him. We've got to time this right. If the train stops and we're not in there to nab him, he'll get away to kill a lot of people."

Winnie nodded assent and moved forward. An older man pushed open the door for her. Winnie moved right behind him shaking out her now unsequestered hair.

Somehow the man in front seemed vaguely familiar. *Was it the cologne he wore? No, it's the clothes. I know those clothes. And I think I remember that maroon derby.*

The man turned slightly, revealing a bright yellow vest and narrow hot pink tie under his open, full-length, camel coat. She was stunned for a second and continued her forward movement under Nesbitt's nudging.

The derby man's mouth opened in wordless surprise.

"I can't talk to you right now, Dr. Potts. I have urgent business in the next car." She waved the fingers of her left hand at him. "I like your hat."

Nesbitt turned to stare at Potts, leaving Winnie's undies exposed.

Potts' eyes widened as he took in Winnie's rear view. "Oh, dear, red polka dots!"

Winnie slapped the flat switch that opened the door to Shahidi's car. There was ample space ahead as most of the crowd concentrated at the central exit door when the train slowed for the next stop.

⤴

Shahidi clung to a floor-to-roof silvery pole as passengers pressed by him to join the sardine pack at the door. A mechanical voice announced arrival at the next station as the car slowed to a crawl, "The next stop is Canal Street. The next stop is Canal Street and Chinatown."

Chinatown? I have never been to this New York City part. Perhaps I shall stay on the train. At this thought

Shahidi heard a loud sneeze and several passengers saying "God Bless you Sister" to its originator. Invoking God for such a trivial exhalation was beyond Shahidi's understanding until he saw a woman wiping her face with her upper black robe thereby exposing Nesbitt.

Shahidi touched his worry beads through his pants pocket and praised Allah, *thank you Allah for the warning. I shall exit here to this Canal Street.*

He moved along with the throng, many of whom were Asians. There was still clear cold daylight air left in the day. Shahidi was not, however, anticipating the large merge of people walking about the sidewalks. The cold air was thick with the odor of fish. He looked to his right as his direction took him to contiguous stalls of fish partially sleeping in beds of crushed ice. A few of the larger fish called carp, seemed to be still breathing as their opercula and gills gasped for oxygen. He was grateful that the next block gave way to slightly warmer air and the absence of fish smell.

The streets were alive with vendors hawking their wares of clothing items, lady's bags, jewelry, and watches. A haggard-looking man came up to him with an open attaché on a folding wooden stand. The man tugged at Shahidi's sleeve.

"Sir, I have genuine Japanese and Chinese Rolex® watches."

Shahidi shrugged him off and looked behind him. *The woman and Nesbitt are still after me. The woman is pointing at me. I must change direction again.* He moved as fast as he could dodging men and women bargain hunters, knocking over easels, necktie stands, and J-walkers between streets. The odor of fish hit his nostrils again.

◂

Nesbitt estimated they were fifty feet behind Shahidi. There were still a lot of people ahead, making progress forward difficult. Nesbitt knew his way around Canal Street's Chinese section. He gambled that Shahidi did not. He turned to Winnie, "Stay here, I'm going to maneuver him to head back in this direction. Try to hide in the crowd."

She wrinkled her brow, "Hide in the crowd? Are you serious?" Her words were lost on Nesbitt who was closing the distance between Shahidi.

Winnie was startled when an older Chinese man grabbed her shoulder. "Would the lady like a full-length dragon shawl? It would cover your showing parts."

She looked at the gaudy black silk garment with the bright gold and red dragon on its full length. "How much? I only have five dollars on me." She patted her only nun-frock pocket. "I think. Yes, my wallet is still here."

"Ah so perfect, it is precisely the cost of this very fine covering." He seemed to emphasize the word *covering*.

◂

Shahidi looked around the mob of capitalist Americans searching for bargains in counterfeit goods with expensive brand tags. He no longer could see Nesbitt or the girl.

I will go back to the Canal Street station and escape with another crowd before Nesbitt and the woman can find me. He circled back trying not to breathe deeply when the fish aroma returned. There were less people entering the station than were exiting. He didn't see Nesbitt closing in behind him.

With two blocks to go, Shahidi was back at the fish stalls. A lady with long tan hair and wearing a Chinese black silk wrap with a large fire-breathing dragon on it, blocked his path. "Excuse me woman, I must hurry for my train at the station."

"You're going to have to get by me first...Shah..." Her words were cut short as Nesbitt tackled Shahidi.

The two men began hitting and grabbing each other with Shahidi trying to maneuver for a strangle-hold. A small group of people, mostly women, formed a circle around them.

Winnie could feel her pulse in her teeth as she shouted, "Get the police. This man is trying to kill the Priest."

Nesbitt was at a disadvantage in the dress-like clergical garment. Shahidi had his hands around Nesbitt's throat. Nesbitt folded his hands and brought them up between Shahidi's forearms and used every ounce of strength the way his Navy SEAL training had taught him. The hold on his neck finally released and he pushed Shahidi away with his legs.

Shahidi landed on his back by a small pole sign held upright by two bricks at its base advertising, *Kosher Carp for gefilte fish.* He picked up a large brick and stood over Nesbitt. "Now you will leave this life by violence as you caused the deaths of my family." He raised the brick to bring it down on Nesbitt's head as Nesbitt was trying to stand up.

Nesbitt reached down to his short-length boots for his double-edge Ranger knife. It wasn't there anymore.

Suddenly a loud shout brought sounds of fear from the small circle of observers. The noise of the onlookers was broken by a louder, "No you don't. Not to my Priest you don't." Winnie swung a gasping twenty-pound Carp sideways at Shahidi with all the strength her arms could muster. The razor sharp gill slits caught Shahidi on the neck penetrating his left jugular vein and left external carotid artery. Shahidi went down cracking his skull on the curbstone. The brick he held over his head impacted on the back of his head at the same time. A sickening squish-like thud silenced Shahidi and the crowd.

Nesbitt stood up rubbing his black-and-blue throat. He removed his hard plastic priestly collar. "I think this collar saved my life."

Winnie glared at him, "It did not. I saved your life...with this." She held up her not yet dead smelly Carp.

She yelled at the unmoving Shahidi, "How about that, terrorist. You were brought down by the carp that makes Kosher gefilte fish."

The fallen Islamic extremist made no response. They looked at the dying Shahidi. Nesbitt got close to his ear. "This was all unnecessary, Omar. It was your brother Nabil who sent your parents to Paradise along with his own soul. I became a priest to direct my life's purpose under Godly guidance. I see, like your actions show, that being a Christian Soldier or an Islamic Soldier follows a similar path. You were once a holy man and made the choice to be a soldier. I was a soldier and made a choice to be of a holy order."

Shahidi opened his eyes, "My actions were divinely driven Navy man. There is only one God and that one is Allah. Only one religion and that is Islam." His eyes remained open. He did not blink. His breathing stopped.

Nesbitt looked at Winnie, "He's dead. I hope no one else will follow us."

Winnie hugged her fish and moved side-to-side, "Us…you used the word 'us'."

Chapter 42
The Balance of Life

Monsignor Hannon was in his high-back leather chair. Winnie and Nesbitt sat across with folded hands in their laps. Hannon opened a large manilla folder and removed an 8-by-10 letter with a bright red wax seal imprint. The imprint had the crossed keys of the Vatican with the Pope's signature.

Hannon looked at the paper, "I have never received such a letter regarding any priest or member of my staff. In fact, this is the only written paper the Pope has ever personally sent to me. It has something for each of you and begins with an opening statement to me."

Winnie and Nesbitt remained silent.

"First, his holiness addresses me as Bishop Hannon. I've been promoted. I've also been reassigned to a Cathedral in Cleveland, Ohio." He sipped black coffee from a crucifix-decorated white coffee mug. "I'm happy about that. However, it will go on my record that St. Patrick's was under attack during my prelate-ship. It also notes that expenses for damages and the intermingling of the military with the church is sanctioned by the Vatican. The New York Catholic order and our local constituents will not bear any financial burden." He looked up. "It does not condemn nor condone what has transpired but this paragraph ends with, 'Sometimes to turn the other cheek would not be in keeping with the perception of peaceful results that Jesus had in mind'".

Hannon smiled, "I've made a copy of this for each of you." He made eye contact with Winnie. " The Vatican understands that Winifred Dorfinkle is a Catholic with a Jewish name. One day Priests will be allowed to marry. However, this will not happen in our lifetimes. Sometimes, God brings together members of the priesthood to conjoin with their constituents. Such intimate action requires leaving the priesthood and considering alternative Christian sects. It would appear, Winifred and Father Nesbitt, that you two have been thrown together by fate and a Godly message to bring up your own Christian family.

"Father Nesbitt, we've talked about your calling to the cloth. Some of us must be protectors of our order and are in fact hindered and frustrated at the strain and stress of church leadership. His holiness suggests you find your way on this Earth as most humans do. A balance in life is sometimes more important than adherence to a single vocation. A balance of family, church, and self produces more serenity. Yours will be an example of what Jesus foresaw during his lifetime to be preferred to a lifelong commitment to the philosophies of full-time thinkers. The Vatican thanks you for your service, both for the church and for its protection." Hannon put the paper flat on his desk.

Nesbitt spoke, "The Holy Father makes it easy for me. I feel the most at ease I have ever been. There is a direction of faith I have been considering. Captain Craig agrees with my feelings."

Winnie and Hannon remained silent.

Nesbitt took a deep breath, "Such a balance has a place in the military. Chaplains are an important part of protecting one's country and its citizens. They keep the connection with what's important in life. My goal is to remain a devout Christian . My goal includes a family as well."

Hannon leaned forward, "You said devout Christian but not devout Catholic, Father Nesbitt."

"A Christian, yes, Monsignor…I mean Bishop." He smiled and looked at Winnie. "I might find the right woman even while I'm serving my country in the Navy with a Chaplain collar."

Winnie stared at him, "You already found the right woman, Forbish Nesbitt. You know it. I know it. God knows it. In fact God inspired it."

Nesbitt and Hannon stared at her. Hannon spoke, "How did God inspire it?"

"It's obvious, Monsignor…Bishop. First there was my confession that brought Father Nesbitt and I together. Then there were the attempts on my life linked also to the confessional and the Central Park mugger. And don't forget, I was a nun for a while. I mean, not really, but I looked like one. And then there was the fish that saved Father Nesbitt's life. The symbol of Christianity is the cross but also the fish. When I slugged that assassin with the big carp, it saved Father Nesbitt's life and prevented the loss of other lives. The signs from God are definitely there." She turned to Nesbitt, "Therefore, Forbish, and I hope you have a nickname, we have to get married."

Hannon sat all the way back in his chair suppressing a grin. He remained silent raising his palms up.

Nesbitt looked at Winnie, changed his open-mouth to a smile, and reached for her hand, "I accept. I'll be your husband."

Winnie returned the smile slightly reddened, "Oh my God! Really, I mean okay, we'll both have careers and a family. I've already picked out your best man."

Nesbitt became stiff in his chair, "What? Who?"

"Well, who else, Dr. Myron Potts."

Nesbitt laughed, reached over and held her other hand, "Well, that's a relief. I thought you'd might pick Montague Kelp."

Chapter 43
Annapolis, Maryland

"I pictured this would be a smaller wedding, Forb."
Winnie looked at the crowd approaching the reception line.
"I absolutely love the Naval Academy's chapel. In a way,
it's as beautiful as St. Patrick's and has much more charm."

"Keep talking, I'm getting used to the 'Forb' nickname." Navy Chaplain LCDR Forbish Nesbitt in his man-
darin-collared dress whites, adjusted the ceremonial sword
at his left hip.

Her parents had been ecstatic at Winnie finding a
mate. Her dad was next to her in the line resplendent in his
pink and black velvet lapeled western-cut tuxedo. Originally from Texas, Mr. Dorfinkle still favored western clothing
styles. Mr. Dorfinkle whispered to her ear, "I like this guy,
Winnie. How are you going to fit in your actress aspirations
with his Navy assignments?"

She smiled at Nesbitt and said, "I have one more
year at the Thespian and then no matter where we go with
the Navy, I'll get TV ad commercials while I scope out
Soap Opera parts. I mean little Nesbitts might come along
and change things a little." She touched her dad's shoulder.
"You never know."

Her father nudged her, "Look...over there...the
man with the bright orange tuxedo joining the reception

line, he was Forbish's Best Man. He looks just like Woody Allan from here."

"No dad," she smiled, "That's Doctor Myron Potts. He's my Addictionologist."

Mr. Dorfinkle laughed, "That's my daughter."

Nesbitt nudged her, "Here comes the line. Remember, you're both a Naval Officer's and Navy Chaplain's wife. We must be respectable."

"Oh Forb, you look fabulous in your dress white uniform and sword. And look at all the cadets who showed up. I loved walking under all those crossed swords when we left the church as man and wife. It was a silver and gold arbor-way."

He let go of her hand, "Well here they all come, starting with Captain Craig of Navy Security. Don't forget, be appropriate. Shake hands and smile."

Captain Craig made a slight bow as he extended his hand, "I'm glad we finally meet Winnie, I mean Mrs. Nesbitt. I had my doubts for a while back in New York City. We didn't get Shahidi's photo from the CIA until after you immobilized him with the fish. That's a good sign, if there ever was, that you'll really be supportive to your new husband."

All uniformed Navy personnel and the bride had white cotton gloves. Winnie took his offered handshake, "Captain, can you make sure my new spouse isn't assigned anywhere like the South Pole. I mean, preaching to penguins isn't really a congregation for salvation."

Craig smiled, "I'll guarantee you won't have to move to the South Pole."

Next came familiar faces from her terrorist ordeal at St. Patrick's. A handsome officer shook her hand, "Congratulations ma'am, Lieutenant JG Nelson at your service."

She held on to his hand, "Wait a minute, which one are you S1, S2 or whatever."

"S2 ma'am."

"What happened to S1?"

"He's on patrol with a nuclear sub in Greenland, ma'am."

"Poor guy, Greenland doesn't even have penguins."

Nesbitt nudged her shoulder with his, "Keep the line moving dear. We have thirty cadets who formed our sword covered exit."

After the military came the civilians. They were a mixture of Thespian Drama Academy students and friends, past and present.

Bishop Hannon shook Nesbitt's hand, "Congratulations, It's now Reverend Nesbitt. It seems I've lost two Catholics."

Nesbitt brightened, "But gained two Protestants. We're still a part of the Christian world, Monsignor...I mean Bishop."

Whitney Zotle gave Winnie a hug, "Well, congratulations on your new roommate honey. I'll miss you."

The most stand-out dressed part of the wedding party approached the bride and groom. Dr. Potts in his bright orange tuxedo, chartreuse ruffled shirt, and purple cummerbund complimented his wife's pale yellow chiffon-over canary yellow satin. They exchanged handshakes and gave them big smiles. As the stately gentleman spoke, his Adams apple caused his purple bow tie to bob up-and-down. "Well done, my dear. I trust you will remember the sterling tenet of proper body physiology as you two go through life."

"Oh, Dr. Potts and Mrs. Potts, I thank you so much for everything." Winnie gave him a hug.

"No thanks needed my dear, I was your husband's Best Man, after all. For a while he was the guardian of my existence on that subway car." Potts vigorously shook Nesbitt's hand.

A comely lady dressed in light green added, "At least you didn't end up with a last name like Pickles." Mrs. Pickles introduced her short thin bearded husband, "This is Kurt."

The line finally came to its last witness to their nuptials. He was probably the largest man Winnie and Nesbitt had ever seen in a formal blue-plaid tuxedo.

"I will never forget either one of you. Good luck, sir…and to you also Winnie." The man who looked like a gorilla in formal dress gave them both a crushing hug at the same time.

Nesbitt prolonged a handshake, "Monty, you saved a lot of lives that day, including ours. We'll always remember you."

Winnie's parents recoiled as Montague Kelp reached them. They exchanged pleasantries. Mr. Dorfinkle whispered to his wife as Kelp passed. "That's what I thought she might find as husband material in New York City."

The reception was a true gala event resplendent at a function hall on the Naval Academy grounds complete with the Cadet Navy band.

A chauffeured gray Mercedes arrived for their trip to the airport.

"Tell me again, why you suggested Orlando for our honeymoon, Forb?" Her going away outfit was a persimmon pedal pusher and matching sweatshirt with the purple words "Thespian Academy" across the chest.

Nesbitt squeezed her hand, "You said you wanted a Disney World Honeymoon package. You wanted Mickey Mouse and Goofy to celebrate your marriage."

Winnie kissed him, "No, no, no, tell me again the real reason."

Nesbitt was dressed in jeans and a matching jean jacket with a tan checkered western shirt underneath. "Okay, there's a Navy SEAL unit down there in Orlando with a seasoned Chaplain I want to meet."

"That's okay, I enjoyed meeting your parents, by the way. Your mother seemed delighted that you dumped the Catholic church."

"It's no secret Winnie, she became a Lutheran after the Catholic church kept giving them a lot of grief about the kids not enrolling in parochial schools. Her priest said that no matter what, she'd go to hell because she married outside her faith."

"So what happened? What's the big deal? We both converted."

"The deal was that the children must be brought up Catholic or she'd be excommunicated. So my father, who didn't really give a damn about religion as long as a person had one, agreed." Nesbitt smiled at her, "Kind of like you and your family. Your father was Jewish and your mother Catholic." He paused and laughed.

"What's so funny?"

"Your Father, I asked him if there were any religious conflicts. He said no, as long as everyone understood that…." Winnie put her hand over his mouth.

"Let me tell you what he said. I always loved it." Winnie let her hand down. "Dad said their religions would never get in their way as long as everyone agreed that Jesus was never a Catholic. He was Jewish."

Nesbitt laughed again. "Yeah, he was never a protestant either. It makes you wonder why there's so much conflict over religious beliefs."

Winnie kissed him, "I just don't wonder about such stuff. My main concern now is what to wear when we meet Mickey and Goofy at Disney World."

The Mercedes arrived at the airport. A few people congratulated them as they left the car. They pointed to the words "Just Married" on the sides and trunk of the car.

One man did not share the good wishes of the on-lookers. Dressed in a long gray coat, almost inappropriate for the fair Spring day, the bearded man fingered his worry beads. Al Qaeda Commander Nahlid whispered, "Mighty Islam and the words of Allah condemn your killing of the last member of the Shahidi family."

Glossary of Characters

Dr. Mendi Alibahn—Adem Saleen's ENT Doctor
Cornish Bangdot—Thespian Professor
Detective Lt. Norman Bauman NYPD
Sarah Bloom—former high school student and Winnie's old friend
Clement Bonzac—Flenk's Sing Sing cell mate
Judge Roland Buttons—Judge Deuser's replacement
Jason Clancy—Thespian student
Captain Delmore Craig—Navy Central Security
Claudia-Winnie's family orange and red Macaw
Dr. Primo Corella—Navy PTSD psychiatrist
Judge Dewey Deuser—Judge pro-Flenk plea bargain
Lorraine Domena—NYC Stage Director Professor
Winifred Dorfinkle—24 year-old performing arts student at the Thespian Drama Academy
Rodney Ducette—Flenk's assigned lawyer
Malcolm Flenk—Central Park mugger
Nahlid—Al Qaeda commander
Father Forbish Nesbitt—Catholic Priest and former Navy SEAL
CIA Langley Agent Manning Poore—Receiver of ADem Saleem's story
Monsignor Hannon—Prelate at St. Patricks
Montague Kelp—St. Patricks caretaker and bouncer

FBI Agent Peter Pudder—FBI Middle East Agent

Gertrude Pickles—Dr. Potts office receptionist

Dr. Myron Potts—Addictionologist specializing in eating disorders

Zeldina Potts—Myron Potts' wife

Jonathan Ralston—Drama Academy Instructor

Judge Orville Rennett—Judge not favoring plea bargain

Adem Saleem—Arizona Empire StateBuilding tourist

SEALS at St. Patricks—Nathan, Ron, Del, and Hal

Omar Shahidi—Iraqi survivor of Nesbitt encounter

Nabil Shahidi—Omar's brother and Al Qaeda member

Toriba—London student from Somalia

Rebecca Winslow—Winnie's stage name

Ramik Zamir—Suffern Cell contact at safe house.

Whitney Zotle-Winnie's roommate

Novels by Peter Glassman

The Silver Concho–Dr. Jacob Cotter loses his memory in a train accident. Rescued by Comanches, he still thinks he's a hardened gunfighter and bounty hunter. He's marked for death by those who caused the train wreck.

OCEAN CITY HQ–A Navy SEAL convinces the Navy Department and Secretary of Defense that terrorist cells rampant in the US must be destroyed.

BLACKWATER FEVER–A US Senator and three doctors manipulate Wall Street with murder and malaria.

THE HAPPY HAT–A deadly US cartel imports heroin from Vietnam in the plaster casts of orthopedic patients.

MY NAME IS KEVIN–Kevin kills a member of an alcoholic recovery group and becomes involved in a Middle East attack on the US banking industry.

THE DRUID STONE–The power of Stonehenge reaches out to the US to combat the last earthly holocaust by Iran. Can anyone survive?

WHO WILL WEEP FOR ME–A group of college students and a mob-connected friend maintain their bond from high school when one is murdered by the Boston Strangler.

THE ADJUSTMENT CLINIC–A murderous vigilante organization, the FDA and the DEA are after corrupt evil drug company staff who place profits above patients' lives.

THE HELIOS RAIN–An American soldier returns from Afghanistan to San Antonio with unusual powers from a chemical ambush and is pursued by terrorists.

COTTER–Historical novel of a dedicated doctor bringing modern medicine and justice
to 1870s Texas from Yale Medical School.

THE MYOSIN FACTOR–The treatment for Muscular Dystrophy could enhance the powers of an Army. Three countries want it at any cost.

THE DUTY CREW–The last Christmas of the Vietnam War in Queens Naval Hospital hosts an assault by "peaceful" anti-war activists sponsored by Hanoi.

THE EYEMAN–A marine can't turn off the Vietnam War and targets Asians for 15 years after the war ends.

Short Story Books by Peter Glassman

US NAVAL HOSPITAL–Arrows in the Night. A surgeon returns from the war to find his wife unfaithful and takes his bow and arrow to Central Park. One of 8-short stories.

Coffee & a Story.—Short, short stories written by Peter Glassman as the organizer of the San Antonio Writer's Meetup.

The Diogenes Mirror—a short story by Peter Glassman published in A Hundred Voices Vol.2

Coffee and Another Short, Short Story—More short, short stories by Peter Glassman authored for the San Antonio Writer's meetup bimonthly meetings.

Short Stories Published in Periodicals

The Grapevine Magazine—2017-2020

The New English Review Press—2019-2021

Author Contact Information:

Facebook: http://www.facebook.com/pages/Peter-Glassman/327031907361357

Website: authorpeterglassman.com

Peter Glassman: San Antonio, Texas. 2011-Current

Made in the USA
Columbia, SC
27 November 2021

49800105R00148